WITCH ON THE RUN

A BLAIR WILKES MYSTERY

ELLE ADAMS

1

The sun was shining, the birds were singing, and there wasn't a cloud in the sky. It would have been a perfect day, if not for the very drunk elf lying in a bush and yelling at the lake as Nathan and I walked back to Fairy Falls.

When we passed him, Thistle the elf let out a muffled yelp of pain, possibly because the bush in question was covered in pointy spines. Thistle wasn't known for making wise life choices.

"Are you lost?" I asked him. "You can't be comfortable lying in there."

Thistle looked up at me peevishly. "I had an itch I couldn't reach, so as a matter of fact, I'm perfectly comfortable."

"All right. It's up to you." I rolled my eyes and continued towards the glittering expanse of the lake that bordered Fairy Falls. Thick forest gathered on its northern and western shores, while rolling hills lay to the south and east. I'd always felt the town had a storybook-like appearance, and that was particularly true on a clear-skied day like this one.

As Nathan and I walked on, the elf let out a strident scream. "Help! Get me out of here!"

"I thought you didn't want to get out," I said over my shoulder.

"So cruel," he wailed. "You are very cruel to walk past someone in need of your help."

"You just told me to leave you alone," I pointed out. "Unless you want me to get you out of that bush?"

I didn't particularly want to put my hands into a mass of spiky leaves to rescue a temperamental elf whose clothes stank of alcohol, but magic came in handy in these types of situations. When I pulled out my wand, though, Thistle yelped and dove under the bush, further entangling himself in the spiky leaves. "Help, I'm being attacked!"

"I'm not attacking you. Don't be absurd."

"Help! The witch is attacking me."

I raised a brow at Nathan, who strode over to the bushes and reached out, grabbing the elf by the scruff of his neck. Thistle's legs flailed and kicked, but he scarcely got out a yelp before Nathan planted him on the hillside. When his feet touched the ground, Thistle swayed on the spot, almost face-planting into the bush again. "I demand you unhand me!"

"I already did." Nathan lifted his hand to demonstrate. "You're welcome."

And with that, we left the gibbering elf behind and continued to walk towards the cobbled streets and neat houses on the edge of the lake.

"Not the homecoming I expected," I remarked.

"No, but it could be worse," Nathan said. "At least you didn't have to fish him out of the lake."

"Don't give him ideas." This was the first time Nathan

and I had been on a holiday as a couple since the New Year, and I'd known we'd be coming back to a set of fires to put out, but I hadn't expected a drunken elf to be one of them.

As Thistle followed our trail along the lakefront, his out-of-tune singing caused the merpeople basking in the shallows to come and goggle at him. From what I heard of the lyrics, the song told a meandering tale of an elf who fell in love with a human. Hadn't Thistle himself done the same? I wondered if his human girlfriend was aware of how he'd decided to spend his afternoon as I scanned the shore of the lake for my familiar, Sky. He usually came to meet me when I returned from a trip away, but if he'd heard the elf singing, he might have decided it was wiser to keep his distance.

"What're you looking for?" Nathan shielded his eyes against the glare of the sun reflecting on the glimmering lake.

"Sky," I answered. "I thought he might be outside, since it's a nice day, but I guess he's off doing cat things."

I'd asked if he wanted to come with me, but he'd declined for reasons I could only guess at. Being a cat—a fairy cat, in fact—Sky communicated mostly in meows. However blissful it might have been to have a few days of peace, I'd missed my familiar as much as I'd missed the town itself.

"Maybe he finally made friends with my cats while we were gone."

"That'd be nice." Sky tended to ignore other cats, viewing them as beneath him, though in fairness, being a fairy cat made him a little different than the average feline. He wasn't a typical witch familiar either, but he was still mine.

"Thistle—what are you doing?" Nathan addressed the

elf, who'd waded into the shallows of the lake. Given his short stature, the water had almost come up to his waist, and it wouldn't be long before he was completely immersed.

"I'm not sure we can rely on the merpeople to pull him out," I muttered to Nathan. "Thistle, get out of there."

He ignored me and continued to wade into the water. The merpeople, as I'd suspected, gawked and pointed and laughed rather than volunteering to help turn the elf around before he got any deeper.

From the forest, a winged human-sized figure flew over the lake and seized the elf around the middle. Thistle kicked and splashed in protest, but the fairy kept a firm grip on him until she deposited him on the shore.

"Thanks, Ani," I called to his rescuer, recognising her as one of my friends from among the town's new population of fairies.

"Anytime, Blair." She landed in front of the bewildered elf. "Go home, Thistle. I'm sure Argyle is worried about you by now."

"He's still dating that gardener witch?" I whispered to Nathan. "I'm surprised she puts up with him if he does this regularly."

Then again, it still surprised me sometimes that Nathan was willing to tolerate my own habit of landing myself in trouble, and we'd been together almost a year. Speaking of…

"Watch out, Blair." He caught my arm as the merpeople dove back into the water with a splash that would have soaked both of us if Nathan hadn't hastily pulled me out of the way. Most of the water hit him in the back of the head instead, while Ani leapt into flight to avoid being splashed too.

"Oops." I stifled a laugh when I saw Thistle had been

knocked flat onto his back, and he raised a fist and yelled expletives at the lake. "That might wake him up a little."

"Might." Nathan pushed a handful of wet hair from his eyes. "He should be glad nobody was at the town's border. I'll have to talk to Steve about that."

"You want to check in with Steve already?" The grumpy gargoyle was head of the police force in Fairy Falls, which unfortunately meant he had authority over Nathan's security team. No doubt Steve would have invented an excuse to pile a bucketload of paperwork on Nathan's head in protest at his leaving town at short notice, so if I were him, I'd want to avoid going near the police station until the last possible moment.

"I don't *want* to, but I figure I should get it over with," Nathan replied. "Besides, we're near your dad's house, and you wanted to see him, right?"

"True." I did need to see my dad, though the conversation I'd been waiting to have with him would bring down the mood as effectively as a chat with Steve would. Since I'd be back at work tomorrow, though, this might be my only chance. "I'll see you later?"

"Of course." He gave me a hug and kiss goodbye. "Assuming Steve doesn't put me on back-to-back shifts for the next week."

"He can't do that, can he?"

"Nah, he's more likely to drop them on the new recruits. Which is unfair."

I pulled a face. "Your team works far harder than he does. He doesn't even do much crime solving."

"True, but at least it's easy to know who to blame when things go wrong."

"There is that." Steve might be a royal nuisance, but at this point he was a fixture here in Fairy Falls, and the town had been through enough change and upheaval in the past year not to want to shake anything else up. Besides, he at least stayed out of Nathan's way when his team was protecting the boundaries of the town from any meddlesome paranormal hunters who hadn't been invited in.

The original purpose of the town's security was to make sure oblivious humans didn't wander past the warding spells that covered the village, though since said oblivious humans included my own foster parents, I had mixed feelings on the secrecy rules that governed the magical world myself. I'd spent the first twenty-five years of my life clueless about my birth parents' origins precisely because discussing the magical world with regular humans was a big no-no, and the couple who'd raised me hadn't had the slightest idea that I was half witch and half fairy.

Telling Mr and Mrs Wilkes the truth would certainly be bending the rules, but after they'd had a narrow escape from some particularly nasty fairies a few months ago and had ended up having that experience erased from their memories for their own sanity's sake, I'd wanted to bring them into the magical world again on my own terms. Once things had calmed down a little… which might be hoping for too much.

"Hey, Blair." Ani caught up with me as I entered the forest, which concealed the pathway into the fairies' home. "Did you have a good holiday?"

"I did, thanks," I said. "Has Thistle been causing trouble all week?"

"Nah, only the past couple of days," she said. "I had to fish him out yesterday as well."

"Honestly." I shook my head. "How're things going with your new job, anyway? I never asked." I'd helped Ani get the job at the local university campus library myself, but life had been so hectic lately that I'd forgotten to check up on her progress.

"I'm enjoying it," Ani said. "Samuel keeps erratic working hours, but then again, so do most of the students, so it works out. Though I wish he didn't like to sneakily appear behind me when I'm not looking."

"That's vampires for you." The vampire librarian also happened to be dating my best friend, Alissa, so I was doubly invested in the job working out for both Ani *and* him. Not to mention her employment would also work towards my long-term goal of making any sceptical residents of the town see that most fairies were harmless.

I still needed to do some more work in the other direction, though. The fairies remained skittish of most other paranormals and mostly kept to themselves without inviting visitors into their parts of the woods. There was a reason even Nathan didn't usually come with me to visit my dad. While Dad himself wouldn't have minded, most of the other fairies were disinclined to trust both the paranormal hunters *and* the local police on principle, and the fact that Nathan was technically neither of those things didn't erase their understandable wariness around authority figures.

When Ani and I reached the shimmering path that was only visible to those of us with the ability to see through glamour, I snapped my fingers and shed my own illusion. Wings stretched behind my shoulders, and I savoured the chance to exercise my fairy magic for the first time in a while as I glided above the path into the bubble universe the fairies inhabited.

While I could still hear the birdsong in the trees and the crash of the waterfall near the lake in the background, the forest had vanished entirely. Instead, vibrant flowers filled a clearing of neat cottages. I waved goodbye to Ani and knocked on the door to the home my dad had claimed for his own.

He answered a moment later, smiling, and swept me into a hug. As I wrapped my arms around him, I was struck by a wave of gratitude that my dad and I had reconnected after a lifetime apart. It had once seemed like the entire universe was set against that happening, and even after I'd learned of his existence, I'd been resigned to never seeing him in the flesh. Dad had been incarcerated in the Lancashire Prison for Paranormals for a crime he'd never committed after having spent the early years of my life on the run following my mother's death at the hands of the paranormal hunters. That he now lived in a cosy cottage in a veritable paradise was nothing short of a miracle.

I followed my dad into the living room and settled in one of his comfy armchairs. He perched on another, his own wings folded neatly behind his back. He and I shared the same dark-brown hair and pointed ears, though like all the fairies I'd met, my dad looked much younger than his actual age. I often forgot he was probably older than the town itself; while half humans like me had a regular life span, he and the other fairies were as everlasting as footprints on the surface of the moon.

"I take it you had a nice break?" Dad asked me. "I hope you enjoyed a bit of peace."

"I did, yes." Nathan and I had left in enough of a hurry that I hadn't had time to say more than a quick goodbye to Dad and the others, but it had been one of our last chances to get away before the next inevitable storm hit the town. "How're things here?"

"Quiet."

"Only because I wasn't here." I grinned. "It's all right, you can say it. I'm the one who brings chaos with me everywhere."

"Not at all, Blair." My dad shook his head, curtains of

long hair falling to either side of his face. "It was quiet when you were at the Head Witches' meeting too."

"Which proves my point." The meeting itself had been anything but quiet.

His smile faded. "Yes… we didn't have much time to talk about the meeting before you went away."

"I know." I lowered my gaze, absently fiddling with a loose thread on my coat. Following the coven meeting—which had ended in two people dead and another arrested—it had been revealed that there was a portal into the fairy realm itself in the home of a local coven. While I hadn't a clue how Arabella Knotgrass had obtained the portal, the slightly more concerning issue was the fact that someone on the other side had stolen a Head Witch's magical sceptre from under our noses.

"You told me…" Dad began. "You mentioned a portal into the realm of my kin is currently owned by the Knotgrass Coven. Is that right?"

"Yeah, a portal to Fairyland." I lifted my head to meet his concerned eyes. "I assume that's not the actual name of the place. Or is it?"

"No—there's not an official name for the various realms of the fairies," he answered.

"Various?" I echoed. "There's more than one?"

"Thousands." When my mouth fell open, he added, "It depends on how you define 'realm,' as the fairies' clans are as numerous as your covens and each occupies its own territory. You've seen for yourself that we dislike being pinned down."

I glanced around at the cottage—which was a construction of glamour that had sprung up out of thin air—and saw his point. "There's got to be an actual place on the other side of that portal, though—however you define 'place.' How else can someone have sneaked out and stolen the sceptre?"

"Are you sure that's what happened?" he asked. "I wasn't there, granted, but I would have thought the portal would have drawn more attention if it had been in active use."

"I don't know much about the Knotgrass Coven, but everyone else seemed pretty stunned that they had a portal hidden in their home." I thought back to the confusion that had followed our scuffle with Meredith, the killer who'd been set on obtaining the portal for herself. "The sceptre rolled under the cabinet during the fight, and when the witches came back after Meredith's arrest, it had disappeared. Where else did it go?"

"It's certainly concerning," he said. "I can't speak to the sceptre, but the portal itself… those artefacts aren't easy to get hold of."

"I don't know much about the Knotgrass Coven," I said. "I'm not sure if the portal was originally Arabella's or if she inherited it from someone else like pretty much everything else in that house of hers, but I'm guessing the latter."

"You didn't ask?"

"No. We were in the middle of an arrest, and… and Arabella herself supported the paranormal hunters disbanding the Head Witches." A bitter note entered my voice. "She isn't the kind of person I'd trust with a pathway into the fairy realm inside her house, even if she's never used it herself. Let's put it that way."

Arabella herself might have turned out to be innocent of murder, but she'd been happy to throw everyone else under the broomstick to gain security and power for her own coven. She'd even been willing to look the other way when Rebecca had been mistakenly arrested in Meredith's place, which I wouldn't forget in a hurry.

"Tricky," Dad mused. "The hunters aren't under *his* control any longer, but I don't like the coincidence of a portal being in the home of a coven with connections to them."

"I didn't even think of that." An involuntary shudder ran down my spine at the memory of a fairy I'd be quite happy to never set eyes on again. "The problem is, she kind of had a point about the rules around Head Witches being a mess. The fact that Rebecca ended up being chosen when she's only a kid is proof of that, but if I had to pick an alternative, I wouldn't choose the hunters. Neither would anyone else here."

The fairies had suffered most of all, as they'd been driven out of Fairy Falls by a coalition of hunters and witches and had remained exiled for years until I'd started to help undo the damage. While the witches had generally learned from their mistakes, the hunters lacked that tendency towards self-reflection, and many of them were actively trying to be *more* aggressive towards paranormals in general and not less. There was a good reason Nathan and his sister, Erin, had left their ranks and never looked back.

"True," said Dad. "I'm glad her plan backfired, but I can't fathom what the average witch would *do* with a portal into our realm. It's possible for it to be an unused heirloom, but if she has contacts over there, or if someone is watching her…"

My breath caught. "Who? You mean—him?"

It was a bit ridiculous that I couldn't bring myself to say his name aloud after all this time, as if he were Voldemort, but I'd feel a lot more secure if the hunters' former leader was sitting in a cell and not lurking in the background like a bogeyman underneath the bed. The man I'd once known as Inquisitor Hare had been unmasked as a fairy several months ago and had slipped through our grasp before we could take him to account for his crimes.

For all I knew, Rowe Clearwater had dropped the mask of Inquisitor Hare entirely after being ousted from his position and had gone straight back to being a fairy prince again. I'd initially dismissed that theory, since he'd spent decades disguised as a human and had even gone as far as to persecute the other fairies to bolster his own power. That ought to have excluded him from being accepted by his former allies, but the thought of him hiding behind a portal in a witch's house—a house I'd *been* in—strayed close to the worst-case scenarios that had been brewing in the back of my mind since his disappearance. So did the thought of a powerful instrument like the sceptre ending up in his hands.

No way. He can't even use it, can he? Or could he? This was why I'd needed a holiday, even if I'd only delayed the inevitable.

"I don't know any more than you do, Blair," Dad added. "Nobody has mentioned him recently, but they also haven't spent time in the fairy realms either."

"I wonder if Arabella has?" I drew my arms around myself, goosebumps springing up on my skin despite the warm weather. "If not to meet with the fairies, then to look for the sceptre?"

"I have my doubts. She knows the realm of the fairies is dangerous for humans."

"I guess." Arabella's deal with the hunters proved her unscrupulousness, but the fairies wouldn't agree so readily to help a witch, would they? Not according to my dad, who'd left their realm when he'd met my mother and had been accused of betrayal as a result. The reaction of some of the other fairies to his choice did not promise a warm reception for his half-human offspring, aka me.

Dad hadn't talked much about his former home, but I gathered that it was like the goblin market taken to extremes. Namely, packed with enchantments that played havoc with the senses and ruled by beings who wouldn't hesitate to punish any intruders who dared to enter their lands.

"All we can do is keep our ears open for news," he added. "It's not ideal, but I'm sure Madame Grey is formulating a plan now that she's aware of the portal's existence."

"Yeah." She wouldn't be planning to go there herself, but it was nice to know that our own coven was under strong and clear-thinking leadership. "I'll ask her."

"You're going there now?" Dad rose to his feet. "I know you probably want to catch up with your friends, too, so I won't keep you any longer."

"I'm happy to spend time with you." I did need to check in with Madame Grey, who'd have the news on whether any new Head Witches had been promoted to take the place of the two who Meredith Norwood had killed—and if any new developments had come from Arabella Knotgrass's direction concerning the portal and the missing sceptre. "I'll try to drop by and visit later in the week."

Dad saw me off at the door, and I followed the path out of the clearing into the regular forest. The brightness of the fairies' home faded, and the sound of human chatter reached my ears. I donned my human glamour again with a snap of my fingers before approaching the centre of Fairy Falls. Everyone already knew me as the fairy-witch, of course, but it had become habit to keep on my glamour when in human company.

The witches' headquarters was my first stop, a large brick building that towered over its neighbours. While Rebecca wouldn't have any official lessons on a Sunday, I figured I was more likely to find her here than anywhere else. My eleven-year-old mentee of sorts took some of her magic lessons alongside me, though she also had private tutoring on the matters of being Head Witch from Madame Grey.

Or Aveline Hollyhock. The former Head Witch had announced her intention to give her successor a helping hand, but I hoped Madame Grey had talked her out of it. While Rebecca undeniably needed the assistance of a former Head Witch to help her deal with the responsibilities resting on her young shoulders, Aveline's last visit to town still haunted my nightmares. She'd wrecked my flat, tormented my cat, and driven both me *and* Alissa out of our minds. *Anything but that.*

The lobby of the coven's headquarters was deserted, nor did I find Rebecca in any of the classrooms, while Madame Grey didn't answer when I knocked on her office door at the top of the staircase dominating the ground floor. Maybe she'd taken the day off. She deserved the break, far more than I had, but it was more likely that she'd been called out on some errand or other. The head of the town's lead coven was in high demand.

After another circuit of the lobby, I reluctantly left. I'd have to talk to Rebecca tomorrow and see if she'd got any further with her decision concerning her future as Head Witch. Nobody wanted her to keep the title, but it was Rebecca herself who'd have to make the call, and it was anyone's guess how events would play out now that Aveline had stuck her wand in.

All right. I'd have a quiet evening in with Alissa instead. The two of us lived in one of the ground-floor flats in a property owned by Madame Grey, a grand Victorian-era house that would have been far outside my budget in any other circumstances. Being best friends with the coven leader's granddaughter had its perks.

The first thing I saw was my suitcase, which lay upside-down near the fence. I'd magically sent it home before Nathan and I had left the hostel, so it was a miracle that it hadn't landed in the middle of the lake instead. Transportation spells were not my strong point.

After grabbing the suitcase and flipping it the right way up, I pushed open the door to the house and fumbled in my pocket for my keys. I unlocked the door on the right-hand side and entered my flat.

"Hey, Alissa…"

The words left my mouth before the sight before my eyes fully sank in. Aveline Hollyhock sat on a sofa that wasn't mine, in front of a roaring fireplace we didn't own, while Alissa herself wore the resigned expression of someone anticipating a march to the gallows.

You have got to be kidding me.

2

I took in the details of my flat's transformation. Alissa stood in a defensive position in the corridor leading to our bedrooms—possibly to prevent our unwanted guest from intruding any further than she already had— while Aveline Hollyhock sat comfortably on the sofa as if she owned the place and the two of us were just visiting. I hadn't a clue what she'd done with our actual furniture, but at least I'd solved the mystery of where my cat had disappeared to. No doubt he'd fled as far from Aveline as possible.

I cleared my throat. "Aveline. Is there a reason you're in my flat?"

"Yes," she said. "I needed somewhere to stay while I trained the new Head Witch, and the other offerings of accommodation weren't to my liking."

Seriously? Yes, our flat was modern and spacious and equipped with everything even a fussy elderly witch could possibly want, but I'd have thought Alissa would put her foot down at the idea of our personal space being invaded by the world's worst house guest for the second time in a year. It was small comfort that Aveline didn't have a sceptre for anyone to steal this time.

I took in a measured breath. "Alissa, can I talk to you alone?"

Alissa sprang across the room as if she'd been hoping I'd ask, and once outside the flat, we closed the door on Aveline. I indicated the unoccupied flat opposite ours. "Why couldn't she stay in there?"

"Aveline's allergic to the lavender outside the windows, remember?" she said in an undertone. "I offered to remove it, but she insisted the smell lingered and made her nose itch. Also, she can't climb the stairs."

"That I remember." Every minute of her past visit was etched into my memory for eternity, unfortunately. "You know, when she said she wanted to train Rebecca, I didn't know she'd be staying in Fairy Falls. Let alone our *house*."

"Neither did I," she said. "My grandmother and I tried convincing her to stay elsewhere, and we must have tried out every single inn and hostel in town. She rejected most of them for being too close to the lake and the other half for other petty reasons."

"What's not to like about the lake?" My jaw twitched. "Also, who'd she steal the furniture from?"

"She didn't steal it," she answered. "I asked for donations at work when she claimed our own furniture wasn't good enough for her, and I think my co-workers at the hospital felt sorry for me."

"They aren't the only ones, I bet." Not that anyone else was lining up to volunteer their *house* to the most ungrateful lodger on the planet. "How many days has she been here?"

"Since the day after the Head Witch meeting," Alissa said. "I didn't text you because I figured you'd be happier not knowing."

"You aren't wrong." It would definitely have ruined my

mood during my holiday with Nathan if I'd known Aveline was in the process of gleefully taking apart my flat while I was gone. "I'm going to regret asking how long she's staying for this time, aren't I?"

Alissa winced. "Nobody knows, including her. Though if it's any consolation, I don't think she's finding it as easy to cast spells without her sceptre."

"I have no sympathy." How was I supposed to get ready for work tomorrow with her sleeping in my room? I could stay at Nathan's, but it was ridiculous that a grown woman of eighty-seven had never learned the concept of boundaries. "Will you be okay if I stay with Nathan for the duration? I know it's not your room she's staying in, but she's taken over the living room and I can't imagine it's fun to listen to her snoring either."

"Earplug charm," she reminded me. "Really, the worst part is when I come back in the early hours from a shift. *She* doesn't wear an earplug charm, and if I wake her up, she harangues me for keeping an old lady from her rest. Poor Roald has been hiding under the bed for the past day."

"And Sky?"

"He coincidentally vanished the day she moved in."

"Figures," I said. "I'm surprised he didn't pee in her shoes or put mice in her bed."

My cat was pretty independent, but he'd had a rough time during Aveline's last visit, and I didn't blame him for making a quick getaway.

"I'm sorry you had to come home to this, Blair," said Alissa. "My grandmother is irked with her as well, but if she hadn't offered her suitable accommodation, Aveline would have withdrawn her offer of tutoring Rebecca."

"I thought Rebecca didn't *want* to be Head Witch." She

hadn't told everyone yet, but I figured Madame Grey would have passed on word to her granddaughter of our discussion after the meeting. If there was any loophole in the rules allowing Rebecca to give up the sceptre, Aveline would know, but she shouldn't need to camp out in my room for an unknown period of time in order to pass on a single piece of information. *What is Madame Grey playing at?*

"You'll have to talk to my grandmother if you want to know the rest," said Alissa. "I think she's paying house calls to the leaders of the other local covens today, but she'll be back later."

"Good. I wondered why she wasn't in her office." The other covens were no doubt full of questions concerning the recent Head Witch meeting too. "You aren't staying in here for the rest of the day?"

"Definitely not," she said. "I was waiting for you to get home, so you didn't have to face her alone."

"Cheers." It was a small consolation, but one I was grateful for. "Let me guess… you're going to hide out at Samuel's place?"

"Until my shift, yes. I might take Roald with me. He doesn't like the noise, but anything's better than staying here."

"Yeah, even being surrounded by rowdy students is better than being in Aveline's company." At least Alissa had the option to stay with her vampire boyfriend at the library on the town's only university campus, but she didn't deserve to be shoved out of her own flat. "I'll look for Madame Grey on my way to Nathan's place."

"He's talking to Steve?" she guessed.

"I'd almost pick him over Aveline." I glanced behind me at the door, hearing the crackle of the fire in the background. "How can she stand the heat in there?"

"No idea. I was hoping she'd slowly boil and evaporate."

"Wouldn't that be nice." I picked up my suitcase and nudged open the front door.

As I left the house, I nearly jumped out of my skin when Aveline herself stuck her head out of the window to my flat. *That would explain how she can still breathe in there with the fire on.*

"Leaving already, are you?" she asked. "I'm insulted."

"I'm staying at my boyfriend's." I continued to wheel my suitcase down the garden path.

"Boyfriend, you say?" Her expression brightened. "The hunter one?"

I groaned inwardly. *I knew I shouldn't have said that.* "Not a hunter. He works for the town's security team."

I did not want her to meet him face-to-face again, not after her nightmare-worthy attempts to flirt with him during her last visit. From her grin, she remembered, too, but I did my best to ignore her cackling in the background as I fired off a message to Nathan explaining that I'd temporarily lost access to my flat. He wouldn't mind me staying with him for a while, but it was my cat I was worried for. Sky didn't tend to get on particularly well with Nathan's own cats, and for all I knew, the mere notion of Aveline staying in town had caused him to permanently move in with the elves in the forest or something.

Right. I have to find Madame Grey.

Luckily, the woman herself must have guessed the timing of my return. As I wheeled my suitcase up the high street, I spied Madame Grey walking towards the witches' headquarters with an imperious stride, her spectacles gleaming in the sunlight.

"Blair." Madame Grey halted in front of me. "You're back earlier than I expected."

"I was going to look for you, but you weren't at your office." I faced the elderly leader of the Meadowsweet Coven and reached for my mental list of questions, but the one that came out first was, "Could you really think of nowhere to put the former Head Witch that wasn't in my flat?"

Aveline might be utterly unbearable, but Madame Grey ultimately held more power and influence in the town, and you'd think she'd have had the final say, especially when she owned the property herself.

"I'm sorry, Blair," she said. "If her daughter had come with her, there might have been other options, but Aveline isn't as strong as she used to be, especially without the sceptre."

She's strong enough to make a royal nuisance of herself, evidently. "I know you tried all the other options, but do you really not know how long will she be there?"

"As long as it takes Rebecca to catch up on her Head Witch training," said Madame Grey.

"I thought Rebecca wanted to quit." I spoke in a low voice, wondering what had driven Madame Grey to conclude that the best thing to do to a traumatised eleven-year-old was to hand her magic lessons over to a woman who hated animals and used a dangerous magical object as a walking stick. "Also, is it up to Aveline to judge whether Rebecca meets the standards of a Head Witch? She had decades of training, and Rebecca's only had a few months. It's hardly a fair comparison."

"You're telling me what I already know, Blair," she said. "I'm doing my best, but the recent upheaval involving the Head Witches has had far more severe and far-reaching consequences than your living arrangements."

My face heated. "I didn't mean to imply there weren't

more important issues. I'm concerned about Rebecca, not myself. She's been through enough already."

I'd had reservations about leaving town so soon after Rebecca had almost been jailed for a crime she'd never committed, but she'd convinced me to go. Besides, as I'd pointed out to my dad, trouble tended to follow *me* around, not her.

"She's fine," said Madame Grey. "She was a little shaken after the events at the meeting, but she's been able to settle back into her routines without any issues. Aveline is training her twice a week, but she still has regular magic lessons with Rita."

My shoulders relaxed a little. "To be honest, if I was offered the choice between jail and lessons with Aveline, I'm not sure which I'd pick."

"Really, Blair." Her lips compressed. "Aveline is… troubled. Losing the sceptre affected her greatly, but there's no doubt her inside knowledge of the Head Witches' rules is unparalleled."

"She's teaching theory classes?" That might help Rebecca's case if the other Head Witches objected to her decision to give up the sceptre, but that shouldn't mean a weeks-long visit. "Or is she hoping to live vicariously through Rebecca, since it's the only way she can get close to the sceptre now she isn't the wielder?"

"That may indeed be why she's so insistent upon instructing Rebecca," Madame Grey agreed. "However, the pertinent question among the other Head Witches is the matter of who will replace Meredith and her two victims."

"They haven't been replaced yet?" That might explain why Rebecca had yet to resign her post, since the region didn't need to lose yet another Head Witch. "Meredith's sceptre…"

"It's still missing, yes," she said. "However, the other two have been returned to their respective regions while the covens decide on the potential candidates for their replacements."

I grimaced. "I guess they have to make sure the sceptre doesn't go to someone like Meredith again too."

"Exactly," she said. "Her actions were reprehensible, but so were those of Arabella Knotgrass. However, it's difficult to know the intentions of every candidate, especially ones who hold their loyalties close to the chest."

"Can't you use magic to sense dishonest intentions?" I asked. "A truth potion, or…"

Or something like my truth-sensing ability. I could tell truth from lie in almost all circumstances, an ability that was sometimes inconvenient but also had saved my life numerous times. Not that I wanted to volunteer myself to vet every single potential Head Witch, and they'd never let an outsider muscle in on their traditions.

"There are ways," she said. "However, I can only advise and guide the rest of the council. I can't pick the next Head Witches for them."

"And they can't replace Meredith without the sceptre," I added. "Unless they want to throw all their traditions out the window."

Personally, I didn't think that was the worst way to resolve the issue, considering the sceptre itself didn't do any decision-making, but it wasn't up to me. In any case, between the reminders of the madness I'd left behind, Aveline's invasion of my room, and the prospect of work tomorrow, I already needed another holiday.

~

I WOKE up the following morning with a sense of impending doom, though that might have been because Sky had just coughed up a hair ball on the pillow next to my face.

"Thanks, Sky," I said, voice thick with sleep, and reached to pet him. "Ah—wait. Sky? You're back!"

"Miaow." He pawed at my leg, while I sat up, relieved that he hadn't run away from town after all. After he'd failed to show up the previous night even after I'd left a bowl of his favourite food and some tantalisingly un-popped Bubble Wrap outside on Nathan's doorstep, I'd been worried I wouldn't see him at all until Aveline had departed Fairy Falls.

I scooped the little cat into my lap and snuggled him, ignoring his disgruntled meow. "Nice to see you too."

"Miaow." He began making warning coughing noises again, so I hastily put him down and went to clean up the hair ball he'd coughed onto Nathan's side of the bed. At least Nathan hadn't been in it at the time, since he'd been put on the early morning patrol shift. As we'd discussed at the pub the night before, our suspicions that Steve would be waiting with a small mountain of work for him had proven correct.

Nathan had been far more annoyed at Aveline's pres-ence inside my flat than at the grumpy gargoyle's attempts to make his life difficult, though, and I'd had to talk him out of confronting her in person. While I remained irri-tated at the former Head Witch, I was glad I had my cat back—and Sky evidently felt the same, because he attached himself to my leg when I tried to leave for work.

"It's all right, Aveline won't come here while I'm gone." I delicately pried him loose from my ankle, wincing when his claws snagged my skin. He wasn't usually clingy, but my absence coupled with Aveline's arrival had doubtless knocked him for a loop. Poor thing. "I'll give you lots of attention later, okay? Look, Nathan got you some Bubble Wrap to destroy. You can entertain yourself with that."

Sky liked Bubble Wrap almost as much as I did, but he gave a mew of disinterest when I pointed him towards the pile in the hallway from the day before. While my boss was fairly lenient, that didn't mean I'd be allowed to bring my cat to work with me, so I reluctantly closed the door on him.

Not that Eldritch & Co was a typical working environment—as evidenced when I walked into the reception area by the sound of the office printer snarling like a werewolf. At least I assumed it was the printer and not one of the two *actual* werewolves who worked there. Callie, the receptionist, greeted me in the form of a blond woman and not a wolf, though my paranormal-sensing power always reminded me of the furry face that lay beneath her smile.

"Hey, Blair," she said. "Had a good holiday?"

"I did, yes." The snarling grew louder, emanating through the closed door to our office. "What's going on in there?"

"Lizzie tried to change the printer's ink."

"Uh-oh." Steeling myself, I pushed open the door to the small office I shared with my three co-workers.

In the corner, Lizzie leaned over the printer, having acquired a rainbow streak in her braided hair that I might have taken for a fashion statement if not for the identical streaks on the wall and on the desk, behind which Bethan and Rob crouched. When I entered, the printer coughed in my direction, and a blob of rainbow-coloured ink splattered the wall next to my face.

"Oh no!" Lizzie spun around. "Sorry, Blair."

"Quiet morning, is it?" I rubbed the side of my head

and unintentionally transferred the ink to my wrist and palm as well. "Nice to see you all again."

"Hey, Blair." Rob, the second werewolf in the office, lifted his blond head from his hiding place. "I made you coffee, but I think it has paint in it."

"I'll pass." I ducked as the printer spat another mouthful of neon paint across our desks. "What did you put in there, Lizzie?"

She crouched beside the printer again, her wand in her hand. "I tried a new brand of ink. I don't think it's a fan."

"I wonder what gave you that idea?" I joined the others in hiding, though not before I acquired another streak of paint on my left arm to match my right. A simple cleaning spell would take care of that problem, which was fortunate because I'd have no access to my own washing machine for a while and I didn't want to get paint all over Nathan's house.

Compared to wrangling Aveline, dealing with a cranky printer was child's play. Once Lizzie had stopped it from spitting ink everywhere, we returned to our seats, and I soon settled back into the rhythm of making calls and sending emails to clients. Dritch & Co was open to helping any paranormals find their ideal employees, but I'd recently taken on the responsibility of helping the local fairies find placements with employers that were open to hiring people a little different than the norm. Given my own experience, weird and different were right in my wheelhouse, and I was glad to help the fairies out.

Partway through the afternoon, Veronica came wandering into the office. My boss was almost a mirror image of her daughter, Bethan, except with silver-white hair and slightly older features, and she gave me one of her vague smiles. "Ah, hello, Blair, I'm glad to see you're back. Did you have a nice break?"

"I did, thanks."

"I like the pink in your hair."

"Ah, that was the printer." We'd done our best to clean up the mess, but I must have missed a spot. Next to me, Bethan stifled a grin, but I noticed she had a pink streak of her own across her chin.

"Really." Veronica surveyed the room and then returned her attention to me. "I'd like to talk to you in my office later, Blair. It's not bad news, don't worry."

I was sincerely glad she'd added the last part, or else I'd have jumped immediately to the conclusion that I was being fired. Yes, I'd only been back at work a day and I didn't *think* I'd done anything wrong, but old habits were hard to break. This was the longest I'd lasted in a single stretch of employment, after all, which was a stark contrast to my failed attempts to keep a job in the normal, magic-free world.

Despite Veronica's reassurances, I was a tad distracted during the last part of the workday, especially as Bethan didn't know what the boss wanted me for. After the others had left, I approached the door to Veronica's office with some apprehension. Taking in a deep breath, I knocked.

"Come in," called Madame Grey. I did a double take at her voice and then another when I opened the door to find the leader of the Meadowsweet Coven sitting behind a plain wooden desk. Veronica, meanwhile, hovered beside a filing cabinet, looking somewhat perturbed.

"Madame Grey?" I entered, closing the door behind me. "What are you doing here?"

Veronica usually turned the office into a picnic table on sunny days like this, and the sparse furniture and blank wallpaper were a contrast to the usual eccentricities. I became abruptly conscious of the pink streak in my hair as I approached the desk.

"I needed to talk to you, Blair," said Madame Grey. "Urgently."

"Erm... why?"

"The cabinet containing the portal in the Knotgrass Coven's house has been stolen," said Madame Grey. "Arabella Knotgrass wants to talk to you."

3

I stared disbelievingly at Madame Grey. "The portal to the fairy realm is missing? Since when?"

"Since this morning," she replied. "That's what we believe, anyway, since its absence wasn't discovered until at least an hour afterwards."

"The thief must have been stealthy." Though I had a more pertinent question. "Why does Arabella want to talk to *me*? I've been here the whole time, so if she thinks I pinched it for a quick trip into the fairy realm…"

"She doesn't suspect you of the theft," said Madame Grey. "Though the thief seems to have sneaked in while Arabella was meeting with the potential Head Witch candidates to replace those who lost their titles."

"Then why does she want to see me?"

"She didn't say," said Madame Grey. "I can hazard a guess, but I'd like for you to make up your own mind as to whether you want to come and talk to her."

If Arabella didn't suspect me of swiping the portal myself—and I couldn't count on her not changing her mind when she had me cornered—then either she'd asked me to come because my lie-sensing powers had helped unmask a killer in her home the other week or because I was the only fairy she knew of. I didn't think either of those things was good in the eyes of someone who'd tried to forge a deal with the paranormal hunters. Whether she'd personally known the Inquisitor or not, I didn't trust her.

On the other hand, I couldn't deny my interest in both the portal and the realm that lay beyond its boundaries. Most of my living family were there. "Who might have stolen it, though?"

"That's what we'd like to know," said Madame Grey. "As the break-in was discreet and the thief left no traces, there is no obvious person to blame. The culprit presumably used magic to get in and out of the house, and while the knowledge of the portal's existence used to be restricted to Arabella's coven, word will have spread after the meeting revealed its presence in her house."

True. There'd been over two dozen people at that meeting who might have told anyone they knew, and the covens' capacity for gossip was unmatched. Added on top of the fact that Arabella had tried to subject her fellow witches to leadership under the hunters, it was unsurprising that someone had retaliated against her. The question was, who? And why had they wanted the portal?

"I don't know that I'm going to be much help," I admitted. "The witches who attended the meeting came from all over the region, and without a list to narrow it down, I wouldn't know where to start. Also, are you sure she wants my help and not to accuse me of stealing it myself? What if she's waiting for me with a group of hunters?"

"Blair has a point." Veronica spoke up from behind Madame Grey. "Given past events, I'd be wary too."

"I asked if she intended to make an unfounded accusation, and she said no," Madame Grey said. "Also, I intend to speak to her myself."

That assuaged some of my doubts, and to be honest, being accused of a crime myself was a small concern compared to the knowledge that the portal was potentially in the hands of someone with nefarious intentions. *Who, though? A witch… or a fairy?*

If I declined, I might never find out the truth… and if the thief turned out to be hostile towards the fairies, the consequences would rebound upon Fairy Falls sooner or later.

"All right," I relented. "I'll come and talk to her."

"Good." Madame Grey stepped out from behind Veronica's desk and strode out of the office, her black cloak sweeping behind her.

"Good luck, Blair." Veronica returned to her desk and snapped her fingers. Her office turned into a summery field, complete with flowers and butterflies, as if the brief redecoration had never been present.

As Madame Grey swept past a bemused-looking Callie, I hurried to keep pace with her. "If the theft took place this morning, why did you wait until the end of the workday to tell me?"

"It took some time to confirm the events and to learn that Arabella wanted to talk to you," said Madame Grey. "As you rightly pointed out, there was a chance she might have meant to retaliate for your actions against her the other week."

"By what, accusing me of stealing her portal?" I'd have had a hell of a job smuggling a giant cabinet out of her house and all the way to Fairy Falls, and with an ex-Head Witch lodging in my flat, I didn't exactly have an abundance of hiding places either. "She's the one who wanted to take the Head Witches apart, so I'd hardly be first in line for revenge if I was so inclined."

Unlike Meredith, Arabella had committed no crimes in the legal sense, so she'd escaped with little more than a loss of dignity after her intention to team up with the hunters had come to light.

"I know," said Madame Grey. "Hence why I'm approaching this matter with caution. However, the portal is an artefact with the potential to pose a great risk to the magical community at large, and for that reason, she might be willing to go to any lengths to get it back."

"Which explains why she'd ask for my help."

"Correct." Madame Grey pulled out her wand. "Are you ready?"

Nope. I was hoping for a quiet evening at home. "Ah—have you told Rebecca? I still haven't had time to properly talk to her since the meeting."

"I have not," she said. "However, I doubt she wants to come to see Arabella Knotgrass."

"Yeah… of course." I wouldn't blame Rebecca for not wanting to set foot near the Knotgrass Coven's house ever again. I wasn't enamoured with the idea either, but with reluctance, I followed Madame Grey's lead and pulled out my wand.

Transportation spells still weren't my favourite method of travel, as they required me to keep my focus on my destination, and a slight lapse in attention might result in me landing in the middle of a pond. I'd used a transportation spell to get to the Knotgrass Coven's home before, though, so I felt a little more confident when I imitated Madame Grey's sweeping wand movements.

The two of us vanished and then reappeared on the grassy hill leading to the Knotgrass Coven's home. The house itself was unchanged since my last visit, at least from the outside. The large eccentric manor house changed appearance almost as regularly as Veronica's office, as did the maze of hedges and flower beds that surrounded it.

I followed Madame Grey down the sloping hillside and halted outside the gates, where a curvy witch dressed in green peered through from the other side. "State your names and your purpose here."

"It's me, Arabella," said Madame Grey. "I brought Blair to speak to you, as requested."

Arabella's lip curled at the sight of me. "Can you prove your identities?"

Madame Grey raised her wand and made a swirling motion that seemed to satisfy the other witch, but when I pulled out my own wand, she shook her head. "Take off your glamour."

"Take off—what?" I hadn't known she'd even been aware I was wearing a glamour, but she might have read up on fairy magic after recent events. "All right."

I snapped my fingers, and my wings unfurled. Arabella's expression grew even more disdainful as she took in my fairy appearance, but she opened the gate to let us in. Face flushed, I returned to my human form and focused on the garden to avoid looking at Arabella's judging eyes. Fountains and sculptures lay between the hedges and bright flower beds, and a stone stairway led to the house's entrance.

Inside, countless doors lined a wide entrance hall. Some were mirrors, some led to corridors, and the whole place generally had a flexible relationship with the laws of physics. The room Arabella beckoned us into was small, containing nothing but a desk and a few chairs, but the uncomfortable memory of being interrogated in a similar room stopped me from entering. As I hovered in the entryway, Madame Grey gave me an encouraging nod that unfroze my limbs, reminding me that as long as she was with me, I wasn't in danger of being arrested or interrogated again.

"Sit, Blair," Arabella said impatiently. "I expect you have a lot of questions."

"Yes." A positive deluge, in fact. "Do you have any idea who might have taken the cabinet?"

"I do have several ideas, yes," she said. "You must be curious as to why I asked you to come here. We didn't get off to the best start the other week, did we?"

That was a nice way to couch the fact that she'd worked with the *hunters* and that she'd been happy to let Rebecca go to jail if it suited her. She might not have committed any murders, but if not for my personal connection with the fairies, I'd never have taken her up on her offer.

To my surprise, it was Madame Grey who spoke up first. "Let's not dance around the subject, Arabella. For what reason did you drag Blair all the way from her home when she has far more important matters to concern herself with than helping your coven?"

I stared at her, my mouth open. So did Arabella Knotgrass, though she recovered swiftly. "*You* know why I brought her here."

"I'm afraid I don't," she said. "You never gave me a direct answer. I do hope you intend to give one to Blair."

I had an inkling I'd stepped into the middle of an argument I had no part in, but it was me who'd been invited here. Turning to Arabella, I asked, "Do you want me to help you find the thief? Is that it?"

"Yes, but don't flatter yourself into thinking I believe your skills are superior to any other," Arabella said. "The thief, it seems, took the portal with them to Fairy Falls."

"You think the thief was from Fairy Falls?" My heart lurched. "How do you know they took it there?"

"A large cabinet was fished out of that lake of yours this morning," she replied. "An *empty* cabinet. The portal, it seems, was removed."

Someone had dumped the cabinet in the lake? "I was at work. I didn't know."

"Regardless, you found a killer inside my home, so I thought I'd give you the chance to prove yourself again. Those fairies are friends of yours, aren't they?"

My mouth went dry. *The fairies.* She thought the fairies had taken the portal… but why would she ask *me* to help her? Yes, I lived in Fairy Falls and the hunters didn't, but that hadn't stopped them from storming in whenever it suited them. Granted, Arabella might not be aware of Fairy Falls's unpleasant history with the hunters, and I had zero desire to enlighten her.

"Yes—no," I answered, feeling as if I was being quizzed with a series of trick questions. "They wouldn't have stolen from you. I didn't even tell them the portal existed."

I'd told my dad, though. Nobody had been listening, had they? Even if they had, it was difficult to imagine any of the fairies we'd offered homes to invading a witch's home to steal her property and jeopardising their own safety in the process.

Arabella remained unimpressed. "Rumours have abounded since the meeting, and the result is that a valuable heirloom has been stolen from my coven. This on top of the theft of Meredith's sceptre is unacceptable."

Another part of my conversation with Dad came to mind. "Did the person who took the portal come from the other side? Like with the sceptre?"

"That hardly matters," she said. "Whoever the thief might be, finding the portal will lead us to the sceptre."

I had my doubts, considering she'd made no progress at finding the sceptre even with the portal sitting inside her own house, but I refrained from challenging her. If she sincerely believed one of the fairies was responsible for the theft, I might be the only person who could question them without getting the police involved. Or worse… the hunters.

Dammit. Neither the police nor the hunters could see through fairy glamour, which might prevent her from contacting them except as a last resort, but I didn't even know where to start.

"Can I look in the room the cabinet disappeared from?" I asked Arabella. "If a fairy was in there, I'll be able to tell." Fairy magic left traces invisible to regular sight, though that didn't mean I'd be able to identify the thief.

Her mouth flattened. "You may look in the room, but if you are dishonest with me about what you find in there, I'll be displeased."

That was uncalled for. After she'd had the presumption to ask for my help, it would be nice if she'd have a little faith in me to be truthful with her.

"Unnecessary," said Madame Grey. "Blair has no reason whatsoever to deceive you. She came here at your own request."

Arabella huffed. "Nevertheless, the damage my house suffered at her hands cannot be forgotten. I would ask you to be more careful with the ornaments this time, Blair."

That wasn't even me. It was Meredith. Annoyance rose within me, but I held my tongue. I needed to look in that room if either of us wanted answers, and starting an argument would get me nowhere.

Madame Grey and I followed her out of the room and up the grand staircase that dominated the lobby. I'd had to run up here to catch a killer not long ago, and my body tensed when I faced the room in which Blythe and I had fought Meredith with the help of my familiar. The large cabinet had been the only piece of furniture, and its absence meant the room was a blank canvas.

Arabella cleared her throat. "Well? Aren't you going to look around?"

"I will." I stepped into the room, but all I could see with my human eyes was that nobody had cleaned underneath the cabinet in a while. It had left a squarish dent in the carpet, and a flurry of dust stirred up under my footsteps as I walked. The regular kind of dust, not glittering fairy dust. After Arabella's earlier disdain, I had zero desire to turn into my fairy form again, but my human eyes couldn't see anything amiss. *Fine, then.*

I snapped my fingers, feeling my wings reappear, and my eyesight sharpened. Glitter lurked in the corners of my vision, but it could just as easily have come from me as from the thief. I crouched down and examined the cabinet-shaped imprint on the floor, but no obvious traces of magic were present.

I turned back to Arabella, and the stark disgust in her eyes prompted me to snap my fingers and replace my human glamour. "Nothing's there."

"Nothing?" She huffed. "How disappointing."

"If it was a fairy, they would have left more traces," I added. "I don't know how they would have got in and out either. Fairies can't use transportation spells like witches can, so the thief would have had to carry the cabinet, which would be tricky given its size."

"Transportation spells cannot be used on my property," she said. "No exceptions."

"Oh." A witch could have bewitched the cabinet to make it weightless, but it was also highly improbable that they'd managed to fly out without making any noise. Had Arabella told the full story? "Whereabouts were you when it was stolen?"

"In my office," she replied. "There were other witches working upstairs, but I assume you are aware that my house is bewitched to shift its appearance on a regular basis."

Hmm. The spell on her house might have worked against her if it had moved the rooms around and given the thief a clear route out... especially if the thief had been familiar with the way her house's magic worked.

"The rest of your coven didn't hear anything? Have you spoken to them?" Might someone inside the building itself have been the thief? I didn't personally know any of the Knotgrass Coven's other members, and I had to admit the notion of them harbouring enough of a grudge against Fairy Falls to dump their stolen loot into the lake was highly unlikely, but who else could have sneaked around the house without being detected? "Someone must have heard the thief come in, right?"

Her eyes narrowed at me. "The windows were open. If the thief had wings, they wouldn't need to make a sound."

"Oh." I paused. "I know fairies can fly, but I don't think there's a fairy equivalent to a levitation spell, and they couldn't have lifted that cabinet without one."

Granted, my understanding of fairy magic was even patchier than my magical education as a witch, and the latter put me on a level with the average twelve-year-old, but I had a hard time believing a fairy could have hauled a massive cabinet out of an upstairs window, glamoured or not. No, this was a witch's handiwork, I was sure.

Madame Grey cleared her throat. "Arabella, we've

discussed the unlikelihood of a fairy knowing the route to your property. I stand by my claim that the thief is far more likely to be a witch or wizard."

"Fairy or witch, I want them brought to justice." Arabella beckoned me out of the room with a crooked finger. "Let us return downstairs."

From her tone, Madame Grey's words hadn't convinced her, but at least if the supposed suspects were in Fairy Falls, I wouldn't have to set foot in here again until I'd caught the thief. Not that I knew where to begin. Even if I went with the assumption that a witch had been a thief, there were an awful lot of witches in Fairy Falls. She couldn't possibly expect me to question all of them, could she? Admittedly the list of people who might be interested in stealing a portal to the fairy realm—let alone who also might have had the skills to break into a coven's headquarters and steal a heavily guarded cabinet—was small.

At the foot of the stairs, Arabella swivelled towards me. "If you believe yourself incapable of finding the thief, I have other options."

"No—I'll do it." Nothing for it. I'd have to do my best with the little information I had available. "I'll find the thief."

"Come back here as soon as you do," she said. "If I don't hear from you within three days, I'll assume you were unsuccessful."

No pressure, then. I debated asking for another look around the house before I left, but since the rooms rearranged themselves on an hourly basis, any potential evidence was likely to be long gone, if it had ever existed at all.

Then another question hit me. "Wait—if the cabinet was dumped in the lake, what does the portal itself actually look like?"

"It looks like a mirror, of course," she replied. "A mirror framed in gold."

"Like—a pixie-glass?" I recalled the magical device used to communicate across long distances.

"The design is similar," Madame Grey answered. "Portals are bigger, however, and difficult to hide in plain sight. Let's go, Blair."

I gave the entrance hall one last scan on my way out, but the only traces of fairy glitter I saw were my own. While Arabella wouldn't be able to see them, I was torn between shame and vindication that she'd been forced to accept my help despite her evident disdain for my fellow fairies. I didn't need her approval, but what if one of the other fairies *had* stolen the portal? If they'd had a good reason to want to go back to the fairy realm, they might have felt justified in stealing an object that Arabella saw as little more than an ornament. Who knew, maybe I'd have done the same in their place.

Find the thief first. Deal with the aftermath later.

When Madame Grey and I were outside the gate to the Knotgrass Coven's home, Arabella withdrew from sight, and I exhaled in relief. "That was… unexpected."

Madame Grey turned to me. "You didn't have to say yes, Blair, but I understand why you did."

"Was it really found in the lake near Fairy Falls?" I asked. "The cabinet, I mean?"

She inclined her head. "Yes, not long after Arabella reported the theft. I believe it would be a good idea to look for witnesses who might have been near the lake at the time."

"Yeah… the fairies might have seen even if they weren't involved." Certainly, asking if they'd seen any signs of trouble near the lake was far better than accusing them outright. "I just don't want them to get into trouble, espe-cially if the hunters are Arabella's backup plan."

"Yes… I was afraid they might be," she said. "Linda Graham hasn't been in contact with the covens since the incident the other week, but Arabella might feel the urgency is worth the risk."

I suppressed a shudder at the memory. "What do the other Head Witches think of all this?"

"They're likely unaware of the theft, if Arabella hasn't told them personally," she said. "And the only Head Witch in Fairy Falls is Rebecca."

"And Aveline." Though Aveline didn't have her sceptre anymore, and I had a hard job imagining her hauling a heavy cabinet out of a window. "I don't think it's either of them."

Whoever it was, Arabella had given me the responsi-bility of finding the thief. I couldn't screw this up.

4

One transportation spell later and I landed on the lakeside near Fairy Falls. When my feet touched the grassy hill, an angry ball of fluff and claws collided with my shins. "Ow, Sky."

"Miaow!" He swatted at me with a paw and then backed away, hissing at me as if I'd mortally insulted every single one of his cat ancestors.

"Blair, why is your cat attacking you?" Madame Grey asked.

"I don't know." I backed out of range of Sky's flailing claws. "Maybe because I said I'd spend time with him after I got home from work. Sky, I'm sorry, but there was an emergency."

Sky hissed once more and then ran off, while I mentally berated myself for leaving him behind. If I'd brought him with me, I could have sent him to search Arabella's house for clues pointing to the thief. Admittedly, Arabella might have refused to let me bring my familiar into the house, but I didn't have time to console a sulking cat when I had a thief to catch.

"I'll see you later, Blair," said Madame Grey. "Be careful."

I wasn't entirely sure if her warning concerned the thief or my cat, but I blurted a goodbye and hurried after Sky, whose tail disappeared out of sight around a corner of a street near the lakeside. "Sky, come back!"

He ignored me and kept running. There were too many people on the streets to make me comfortable getting out my fairy wings again, so I jogged through Fairy Falls's cobbled streets, wishing I'd worn my Seven-Millimetre Boots to work instead of my regular shoes.

I skidded around a corner and caught sight of the little black cat speeding past the witches' headquarters and out of sight. He wasn't heading back to my flat, was he? Given that Aveline Hollyhock was the current occupant, maybe he planned to crap in her bed just to spite me. *I can't say I'd stand in his way, then.*

As I stopped outside the witches' headquarters to catch my breath, Rebecca walked out with Aveline close behind. The former Head Witch leaned heavily on a walking stick she hadn't carried the last time I'd seen her, but her dark eyes were as sharp as ever. "Where are you running to?"

"My cat." I clutched a stitch in my chest. "He ran off."

"Why?" Rebecca asked curiously.

"Because…" Did she know about the stolen cabinet? If not, she'd find out soon enough, but Aveline's presence stilled my tongue. "Because I said I'd spend time with him after work and then got dragged off on an urgent errand."

Aveline made a disparaging noise. "I told you he wasn't much of a familiar."

"It was a misunderstanding." Now I hoped he *had* crapped in her bed in protest, even though it was techni-cally *my* bed. "Sky helped me catch a killer the other week. He's not useless."

I'd kind of hoped Sky was listening in and would take the compliment as his cue to forgive me, but no such luck. Aveline grunted and stepped around me, her cane tapping on the cobblestones.

"Hang on." If she got into a fight with my cat, I wasn't entirely sure who'd come off worse now that she no longer carried her sceptre. "Did you hear the news? Ah—about Arabella?"

"What news?" asked Rebecca, at the same time as Aveline clucked her teeth.

"Foolish woman," she muttered.

She knew, but she evidently hadn't clued in her new apprentice. Typical.

"Someone stole the—cabinet." I broke off, wondering if Aveline knew the cabinet contained a portal to the fairy realm. She might not, since she'd shown up after the meeting and had missed most of the action, but she'd been Head Witch for long enough that she must have visited the Knotgrass Coven's home before.

"Cabinet?" Rebecca echoed.

"Like I said, she's a fool." Aveline walked on, ignoring my attempts to stall her.

"Did you hear the cabinet was dumped in the lake?" I overtook her slow pace. "Because of that, Arabella thinks the thief came from here. From Fairy Falls."

While I hadn't been able to picture Aveline hauling the cabinet out of the window, she had magic at her disposal, and she might have wanted to retaliate for Arabella's actions the other week. Maybe it was wishful thinking on my part due to my keenness for an excuse to send her packing, but Aveline was the only person in Fairy Falls who'd both been present at the meeting and whom I had no reason to trust.

She also made no secret of her desire to possess a

sceptre again… and there was one *behind* the portal, somewhere in the fairy realm.

"Yes, I expect those fairies would like to get home." She overtook me again, almost thwacking me in the legs with her cane.

"It wasn't them." I stopped my pursuit, deciding that she deserved to find out the hard way if my cat had left any unpleasant surprises in her bed, and returned to Rebecca.

Outside the witches' headquarters, I found Rebecca had acquired more unwelcome company in the form of her older sister, Blythe. My ex-co-worker and former nemesis narrowed her eyes at me from under her spectacles. "Blair. I wondered when you'd show up again."

"Oh, hi, Blythe." I didn't bother saying I was glad to see her, because she'd know that for a lie without needing to read my mind. "Rebecca, were you at a lesson with Aveline? Is she giving you a hard time?"

"No," she said. "I mean—the lessons are going fine, but I was here to talk to Madame Grey. I didn't realise she'd be gone."

"Oh." I guessed Madame Grey must have got sidetracked on her way back from the lake. "I'm sure she'll be back soon. Blythe, did you hear about Arabella's cabinet?"

"No." Her tone carried a hint of finality. "I don't want to hear anything that'll put my sister in danger again."

"I'm not putting her in danger. Rebecca isn't…" She wasn't a suspect, but would it necessarily stay that way? Arabella wasn't a fan of her *or* the fairies.

"I'm not what?" Rebecca raised a brow at me. "I don't need to be treated like I'm five, you know. I'm a Head Witch."

"I know that," I said. "It's your sister who seems to have an issue with me discussing the reason Madame Grey isn't in her office. She and I went to the Knotgrass Coven's home."

A muscle ticked in Blythe's jaw. "You can't keep yourself out of trouble for a single day, can you?"

"Arabella hired me," I retaliated. "Kind of. That's not the point. What was Aveline doing in there if not teaching a magic lesson?"

"Poking around the supplies, I think," Rebecca answered. "She wanted something for her hip pain."

"She's living in the same flat as a healer," I pointed out. "Specifically, *my* flat. Did she happen to mention to either of you how long her visit would last?"

Blythe snorted. "That's what you get for taking a holiday during a crisis, Blair."

"Is there ever *not* a crisis?" I glared at her. "Meredith was jailed, and none of us has a say in who gets chosen as Head Witch next, do we?"

"I meant the sceptre being missing in the fairy realm," said Blythe. "Or did you forget one of your people stole it?"

"*My* people?" After Arabella's unkindness earlier, her words hit a raw nerve. "I've never been there, as you know perfectly well. If you have a problem with me, why not come out and say it?"

Blythe shrugged and beckoned to her sister. "Come on, Rebecca. Let's go."

I opened my mouth to ask what Rebecca thought of her sister's pushiness, but she shook her head slightly as if to warn me not to challenge Blythe while she was in a prickly mood and then gave me an apologetic look over her shoulder. "I'll see you at tomorrow's lesson?"

"Sure." Not that I had time for a lesson. I had three days to question everyone who might have stolen the portal, and as much as I wanted to find my cat, time was of the essence.

I messaged Alissa asking if she was free to meet me by the lake and then headed back that way. I'd start by finding witnesses. While the lake was huge, it was also full of merpeople and nereids and sirens and surrounded by forest inhabited by fairies and elves and shifters. One would think a giant cabinet falling into the water would have caused a stir.

Typically, the first person I saw tottering around the lakeside was Thistle the elf. He didn't look as if he'd sobered up since our encounter the previous day, and he noted my arrival with bleary eyes. "Oh, hello, Briar."

"It's Blair." Had he been talking to old Ava at the hospital, or was he just confused? "How long have you been here? Were you at the lake this morning too?"

"I may have taken a nap over there." He pointed vaguely to the southeast of the lake. I followed his gaze, but the vastness of the lake was such that I couldn't see the farthest shore even on a clear day like this.

"Did you see a cabinet anywhere? It's a big box… taller than I am, and someone left it in the lake." I measured with my hand and then indicated the lake, though it was beyond me to figure out if my words made an impact in his addled brain.

He let out a splutter of laughter. "I think you may have been at the goblin brew yourself, my friend."

"Trust me, I really haven't," I said. "Do you remember seeing anyone hauling a giant box out of the water a few hours ago?"

"Hmm…" He trailed off, a thoughtful look on his face. "I saw strangers pulling a big box out of the water, yes."

"Strangers?" I echoed. "Whereabouts?"

"There." He pointed to the lake's southern edge. "Men with giant boots. Made a lot of noise, they did."

"Nathan's security team?" Thistle wouldn't necessarily know them by sight, especially while intoxicated, but the word *strangers* rang alarm bells in my mind.

No. He can't mean the hunters. Madame Grey would never let them near here.

"Were they inside the town itself?" I followed his gaze across the lake, whose distant edge was little more than a murky line. "Or was it outside of the borders?"

"Too complicated." He yawned. "I will sleep now."

Amazingly, he did, folding onto the grassy hill and drifting off with a single loud snore. At least he hadn't fallen into a bush this time, but his words had unnerved me. Nathan would have told me if he'd fished a cabinet out of the lake, right? I pulled out my phone and fired off a message to him, hoping the elf had been too confused to recognise our own security team.

As I hit send, Alissa replied to my earlier message, confirming that she was free to meet up. Since she hadn't been at work, I figured she'd been at the university campus, spending her free time with Samuel between shifts. Hopefully we'd have more luck finding witnesses with two of us.

Within a few minutes, Alissa met me on the shore. "What's up, Blair? What're you looking for?"

"I couldn't give you all the details in a message," I said, "but a certain portal to Fairyland vanished from Arabella Knotgrass's house this morning, and she's decided the thief is in Fairy Falls because they found the empty cabinet in the lake."

Her mouth parted. "Whoa. Did my grandmother tell you that?"

"Yes—and Arabella herself." I told her the rest as we walked around the lake's edge, keeping an eye out for anyone in the water within hearing distance. As it was early evening, the lake was pretty quiet, though it was possible that all the merpeople had swum off in protest at their water being defiled by Arabella's empty cabinet.

When I'd finished, Alissa shook her head. "The portal is missing, but the thief ditched the cabinet?"

"Somewhere around here." I gestured at the lake. "Thistle the elf said he saw some strangers carrying it off."

She snorted. "I don't know that I'd trust his word. He barely knows one hand from the other even when sober."

"No, but there must be other witnesses," I said. "Even if it was glamoured at the time, water tends to move around when you drop a giant box in it, doesn't it?"

"Fair point." She scanned the lake, shielding her eyes from the sun's bright reflection on the surface. "Does Arabella have any suspects?"

"All the fairies, pretty much." I grimaced. "Which is absurd because most of them didn't know she *had* the portal, and they wouldn't have endangered the rest of us by stealing from a witch as powerful as Arabella Knotgrass."

"She has no shortage of other enemies, but I don't know who in Fairy Falls is familiar with her," said Alissa. "Let alone who'd want a portal into the fairy realm."

"Or a sceptre," I added. "Meredith's sceptre is on the other side. That might be a factor too."

She frowned in confusion. "The fairies can't use sceptres, right?"

"I don't think they can, but remember who's staying in my room?" I gave her a significant look. "She's the one Head Witch, or ex-Head Witch, who's currently in Fairy Falls. Not counting Rebecca, of course, but I don't need to explain why *she* isn't the thief."

"You think it might have been Aveline?" Alissa's eyes

grew wide. "She definitely wants her hands on a sceptre, true, but don't forget she's not as strong as she used to be. I can't see her pulling off a stealthy robbery, can you?"

"I bet she knows the way around Arabella's house," I said, undeterred. "And with magic, anything is possible."

"Why'd Arabella ask you to help her?" asked Alissa. "I thought she didn't like you."

"She doesn't." My cheeks burned at the memory. "She *hates* my fairy form, but she's backed into a corner. The hunters screwed up the last time she hired them, and the regular police wouldn't know where to start."

Alissa grimaced. "I expect it was a tricky decision for her. I don't blame you for feeling obligated to step in for the fairies' sakes."

"She gave me three days before she goes looking elsewhere," I said. "Though I'm not sure how long her patience will hold out."

"Not long, given that her property was stolen." She stood on tiptoe to see across the water. "Hey... there's a mermaid over there."

Alissa lifted a hand and waved at the distant figure. I could theoretically go into fairy mode and fly over to the mermaid, but I was still a little self-conscious after my encounter with Arabella earlier, and sometimes the merpeople got touchy about people flying too close to their territory.

The mermaid swam towards us, her dark hair floating around her in the water as if it were weightless. "You're the fairy witch, aren't you?"

"I am." I shouldn't be surprised that even the folk who lived in the lake all knew who I was. "Did you see someone drop a giant cabinet into the lake earlier?"

"Who didn't?" She flicked her tail, splashing Alissa and me with water. "It fell with a massive splash, like that."

"Did you see who dropped it?"

Her tail flicked again, and I stepped back to avoid getting splashed for a second time. Poor Alissa wasn't so lucky, and the water hit her full in the face.

"Can you not do that?"

"Why not?" The mermaid pouted. "Humans are so boring."

"Did you see who left the cabinet in the water?" I decided to let the insult slide. "Did they use magic to carry it?"

"No, I didn't see them," she said. "The box fell out of nowhere. Sort of like this."

Alissa and I both scooted back as her tail flicked a wave of water over our heads. Pushing tendrils of wet hair out of my eyes, I blinked my eyes clear. "Thanks a bunch."

"You're welcome." The mermaid dove below the water again and swam off with a single flick of her tail.

I rolled my eyes at Alissa. "Now I know why they don't bring in mermaids as witnesses."

"Out of nowhere?" She pushed her damp hair aside, echoing the mermaid's words. "I suppose if the thief was invisible or glamoured at the time, it would have looked as if the cabinet dropped out of thin air."

"I figured." *Glamoured.* That didn't bode well for the fairies, but it was possible for a witch or wizard to use a similar spell to render themselves unseen. "Do you want to go and hunt for the cabinet itself, or look for more witnesses on this side of the lake?"

"The latter," she said. "It won't get dark for a while, so we can find the cabinet later."

"True." With the thief hidden from sight, witnesses would be hard to come by, but if they *had* been glamoured, the fairies might have seen through the disguise.

Nothing for it. I'd have to talk to them directly myself

and hope that if the thief was among them, they'd come forward without a fuss.

As we continued to pace along the lakeside, we passed Thistle's hiding place. Alissa rolled her eyes at his sleeping form as she stepped around him. "He's back, I see."

"Didn't he have a human girlfriend?" I whispered. "I'd have thought she'd be able to talk him out of this sort of nonsense."

Unless they'd split up, which might explain his erratic behaviour in the past day. This was a favoured spot for elves to drown their sorrows, apparently, but I didn't have time in my schedule to ponder elf romantic drama when I had a thief to find.

"You'd think." She rolled her eyes. "I don't see any other witnesses… any ideas?"

I drew in a breath. "I think I should talk to the fairies. They can see through glamour."

"Good call." She nodded. "I'll wait here. They might be more willing to talk to you alone."

"I hope so."

If Thistle had been right and some strangers *had* found the cabinet, then time was more limited than I'd known. Whether the thief was among them or not, I had to warn the other fairies that trouble was coming.

5

―――――――

After Alissa and I parted ways, I entered the forest and made for the path to the fairies' home. With my thoughts preoccupied, ticking over ways to break the bad news, I didn't see the small figure following me until he loudly cleared his throat.

I turned on my heel and spied a pair of brown eyes watching indignantly from amid the bushes. "Erm, hi, Bramble."

Like Thistle, the elf was somewhere under five feet tall and dressed in bark-coloured clothes that blended into the surrounding forest. His pointy ears stuck up through tufts of short hair, and he carried a sharpened stick in one hand. "Why is a human trespassing in the forest, I wonder?"

"I'm not trespassing." What was he talking about? "I'm nowhere near your part of the woods. Besides, I've been to see your king several times, in case you've forgotten."

"You haven't come here in so long that we might as well be strangers," he growled. "The king is greatly insulted by your absence."

"I'm sorry he is. I've had a lot going on." Yes, it'd been a while since my last visit, but I hadn't known the elves' king would take it as an insult.

Wait a moment. Did the elves know about the missing portal? Unlike the fairies, they'd been firmly entrenched in the woods for years, and they also had an ongoing rivalry with the local witches. On the other hand, I didn't see any of them having a particular reason to want to steal from a coven several towns away.

"Yes, you have," he growled. "We know from how you keep bringing your troublemakers into the forest."

"Who?" I said blankly. "Bramble, I have no idea who you're talking about. I didn't bring anyone here."

"The former Head Witch, of course."

"Aveline?" He couldn't possibly mean anyone else. "Believe me, I know all about her tendency to barge into people's houses and make a mess of things, but I didn't bring her here. She invited herself to Fairy Falls in order to train the Head Witch."

"The new Head Witch was appointed on your watch," said Bramble. "You cannot deny that you are the connecting factor and at the centre of most trouble that unfolds in this town."

Harsh, but not untrue. "I didn't bring Aveline here. I want her gone, too, but it's not up to me. Anyway, I have a question. Did you or any of the other elves see a giant cabinet being fished out of the lake earlier?"

He looked at me as if I had a screw loose. "No, we did not. Perhaps that drunken fool did."

"Thistle? He did, but he also doesn't remember very well." I racked my mind for a way to phrase the question that he wouldn't take as an insult. "Did any of you see or hear anything weird this morning?"

His eyes narrowed. "Yes, that ghastly woman was

tramping around the woods again. I'd appreciate it if you told her to stay out of our territory."

Aveline was in the woods? "I'll talk to her. Ah—do you want me to come with you and speak to the king too?"

"Not yet." He made to retreat into the bushes. "I will inform him of your presence here, Blair Wilkes."

Right. I'd been under the impression that the elves didn't want me randomly wandering onto their territory without any reason, and it was news to me that the king thought I'd snubbed him.

When the elf had departed, I returned to searching for the bright path to the fairies' part of the woods. Upon emerging into the grassy clearing, I rapped on the door to Dad's cottage, and he answered with a surprised smile. "Hey, Blair. Wait, is something wrong?"

"Yeah." My gaze swept around the clearing, but none of the other fairies looked twice at me. I didn't believe any of them would have taken the portal, even if they had heard our discussion yesterday, but they certainly wouldn't be happy to learn of Arabella's accusations. "Can we talk somewhere else?"

"Outside? Sure." He closed the door behind him, and we left the clearing for the path leading back into the forest.

As we walked, I gave him the gist of the situation, summarising the theft and the discovery of the abandoned cabinet, as well as my failed attempts to find witnesses near the lake.

"I don't suppose anyone heard or saw anything from the clearing?" I asked as we reached the lakeside, where the sun had begun its gradual descent towards the horizon.

"Not to my knowledge." His expression was grim. "Does this Arabella Knotgrass think you're likely to be able to solve this crime single-handedly?"

"No, but I'm not seeing many other options," I said. "I'm lucky she didn't accuse me of taking the portal myself, but she's adamant that a fairy must have been responsible. If I don't get to the bottom of this, she'll send in someone much less friendly."

"Why did she have a portal to the fairy realm to begin with?" he queried. "Did you have time to ask her?"

"She mentioned it being an heirloom," I recalled. "I don't know anything else, including whether she actually used it herself."

"I have my doubts," he said. "Few humans willingly set foot in the fairy realm."

"I didn't even know it was possible," I admitted. "Does that mean the thief might be inside the fairy realm itself?"

"No," he said. "Generally, portals only work for anyone who's been granted an invitation into the realm that lies on the other side of the mirror. If Arabella Knotgrass inherited the portal rather than being given it as a personal gift, she would be unable to use it."

"An invitation?" I frowned. "From a fairy?"

"Yes, and usually the invitation takes the form of a token gifted to the recipient that enables them to access the portal," he replied. "There's no guarantee it would work for anyone else."

"Really?" It sounded as if Arabella's coven had kept the portal as more of an ornament, which was a little better than the notion that they were secretly meeting up with the fairies in their free time. Besides, given Arabella's disgust towards my fairy wings, I had a hard time imagining her being friendly with anyone on the other side of the portal. "I guess someone in her coven a few generations back must have been friendly with the fairies."

"Likely, yes," he said. "I am unfamiliar with the Knotgrass Coven, but it sounds as if this Arabella worked hard to keep the existence of that portal a secret. If it took scarcely a week for it to be stolen following its exposure, it's no wonder she refrained from telling anyone."

I halted in my tracks. "Do *you* think a fairy is likely to have taken it? Because if no humans can use it without help from the other side…"

"There are others who can use portals," he replied. "Elves, goblins, and any other species related to ours."

"The elves." Wait. "I don't know how much they know about all this, but I can ask. One of them is the only witness who saw the cabinet get pulled out of the lake, but he's also a local drunk."

"Where is the cabinet now, do you know?"

"On the other side of the lake, apparently." I pointed across the water. "Nobody saw who dropped it, because the person carrying the cabinet was invisible or glamoured at the time."

His gaze shadowed at the word "glamoured." "There were no clues at Arabella Knotgrass's house that pointed to the identity of the thief?"

"Nope," I said. "They smuggled it out of the window of Arabella's house without leaving any traces. That or they used the door, but they'd have needed to be familiar with the magic controlling the house to slip around the security."

"There's a chance someone who was present at the meeting a few weeks ago was the thief," he said slowly. "Right?"

"Right, but the only people from Fairy Falls who were at the meeting were me, Madame Grey, Rebecca, and Blythe." I counted off on my fingers. "And Aveline Holly-hock, though she's not local. She's also currently tres-passing in my flat."

"In your *flat?*"

"Yeah, with Madame Grey's permission." I heaved a sigh. "She's the least of my problems, though. I have three days—more like two, really—to find the thief before they send in the hunters."

"I wish I could help," said my dad, "but none of the fairies who currently live in Fairy Falls has any desire to go back into that realm. Certainly, they wouldn't have reason to steal a portal from a human."

"They don't want to go back? At all?" I recalled his paradoxical claim that the fairies' realm consisted of countless smaller kingdoms that fell under the same banner. If the place on the other side of the portal wasn't one the local fairies were familiar with, it made sense for them not to have any interest in going back.

There was still a small chance that someone had simply wanted to take the portal out of the hands of the covens without making use of it themselves, but that was pure conjecture.

"For most of us, our relationship with the fairy realm is complicated." A preoccupied expression came over his face, and the sound of the waterfall filled the silence between us for a moment. "We don't think of it as home. I don't, anyway."

"You said there were thousands of smaller realms, right?" I asked. "Can we find out which part is on the other side of that portal?"

"If Arabella is unaware, it would be difficult to learn without using the portal," he said. "Each part of the fairy realm is as distant and isolated from another as Fairy Falls is from other magical communities. Our home is not a mirror of this world, and its various kingdoms regularly shift around due to the glamour that suffuses the realm. You've seen it on a smaller scale here."

True. The clearing, which had appeared overnight, and

which expanded whenever a new fairy moved to town, didn't seem to belong to the same world as the rest of us did. The fairies themselves had created it from the strength of their magic, and I could scarcely comprehend the same magic on a large scale.

Once again, I was reminded of how little I really knew about the fairies in general. Despite forming half my family, they might as well have been an alien species.

Dad gave me a searching look as if he'd guessed my thoughts. "Fairy Falls is our home now. Whichever realm is on the other side of that portal will be no more welcoming to us than it would be to the average human."

I thought on this. "Might the thief have wanted to get into that particular part of the fairy realm?"

"Court," he corrected. "Or kingdom, each of which is ruled by a particular fairy prince. 'Prince' is just a title, so they can be male or female."

"Like… like Rowe Clearwater." I spoke his name in a whisper, as though the waterfall itself might be listening in. "The Inquisitor. He used to be a prince before he moved into the human realm, right?"

"He did, and I know nothing of the court he left behind," he said. "The fairies take a more fluid view of the passage of time due to our long-lived nature, but it's anyone's guess as to whether any of his former allies remained loyal to him after his long absence."

"I bet they did." People like him always found allies. "What if the person who took that portal wants to use it to help *him*? I mean, he's been on the run for ages, and nobody has caught him yet…"

He shook his head. "Unlikely. Unlike humans, fairies do not require assistance to get into our own realm."

"Then—" I faltered. "You could travel there right now?"

"I could," he confirmed. "I'd be trespassing, however, and the person in charge of that part of the fairy realm would be within their rights to kick me out or worse."

I turned this over in my mind. "If the thief wanted to use the portal, it must have been a human, then."

Dad inclined his head. "A witch who coveted the portal for their own collection, perhaps."

"Or someone who wanted the sceptre," I added, thinking of Aveline.

"Like I said, I'm not convinced the sceptre was taken into the fairy realm," he said. "I'll ask around and see if anyone has been near the lake today, though."

"That'll really help," I said gratefully. "I don't want to accuse anyone, but this isn't like when those kids went missing. This is about an actual portal to the fairy realm, and if anyone from here does turn out to be the thief, the consequences will land on all of us."

With the word "us," I intentionally included myself among the fairies. I might be a member of Madame Grey's coven, but Arabella's reaction was a stark reminder that not all the witches thought of me as one of their own. Besides, I would never abandon Dad and the others to face the hunters alone.

Dad's lips pressed together. "You mean Conor, don't you?"

I sucked in a breath. "I know he had good reason to take the Seeing Stone…"

"Because I asked him to," he added. "He would be displeased to learn that a portal was in the hands of the covens, certainly, but he wouldn't risk the others' safety by stealing it back."

"I know." I dropped my gaze. "I don't want to believe the worst of any of you, but if there's the slightest chance

—I'd rather someone confided in me first than risked the wrath of the hunters."

"I'll talk to Conor myself," he said. "I don't think he even knew the portal existed, but I'll see what he says."

"Thanks." I lifted my head again, glad he understood the urgency. "I don't want to put this on you, but you know he won't take it well if I'm the one who shows up at his door and starts asking questions."

"No… you're right there," he said. "You should head home. It's been a long day for you, hasn't it?"

"Yeah… and I need to find my familiar." I'd forgotten Sky had run off earlier, but if he'd spent the evening tormenting Aveline, it'd serve her right for invading my flat. "And Nathan."

He hadn't replied to the message I'd sent earlier, which was unusual, but maybe he'd been asleep all day after last night's shift. He wouldn't have been able to come with me to talk to the fairies anyway, given their general distrust, but I needed to break the bad news in person.

When I reached the door to Nathan's house, he didn't answer my knock, so I pulled out the spare key that he'd given me and unlocked the door.

A muffled yelp greeted me on the other side. "Ah— Blair? Is that you?"

"Hello? Nathan?" His voice had come from behind the closed living room door, which I pushed inward—and I saw at once why he hadn't texted me back.

Nathan's phone lay pinned beneath a giant paw, while Nathan himself sat with his back to the wall. Sky's monstrous form crouched in front of him, blocking his way out of the room. My small black cat had transformed into a shaggy beast bigger than a sofa, and I didn't blame Nathan for not daring to reach under one of those massive paws to rescue his phone.

"Nathan!" I let the door swing shut behind me. "Sky, I already told you I was sorry for not getting home fast enough. There's no reason to take it out on my boyfriend."

"That's what this is about?" Nathan asked, baffled. "I got your message, but I didn't have the chance to read much of it before Sky knocked my phone out of my hand. That was an hour ago."

"I didn't know you were being held hostage by my cat. Sorry." I attempted to shuffle around Sky's giant shaggy form, but he turned his head away from me. "Sky, you must know I couldn't say no to meeting with Arabella Knotgrass. I was going to come straight home."

"You met with *who*?" Nathan pushed to his feet, with difficulty, and ducked under Sky's giant fluffy tail.

I approached the giant cat-monster. "Sky, please don't blame Nathan for this. He didn't know anything."

"Believe me, I wish I did." Nathan beckoned me onto the sofa next to him, and Sky finally shrank back into his smaller form. I made to scoop him up, but Sky ran for the open door into the hallway.

"Sky, I can't make it up to you if you keep running off, can I?" I sat on the sofa and beckoned him into my lap. "C'mon. You want my attention, don't you?"

"Miaow." He bounded away from the door and crawled onto my lap, pinning my legs down.

"Really, I was going to come straight home as soon as I was done talking to Rebecca." I gave him a stroke. "I hadn't seen her in days, and I wanted to know what that demonic Head Witch was teaching her."

Nathan gave a confused laugh. "I assume you mean Aveline, but why did you have to talk to Arabella Knotgrass?"

"Someone stole the fairy portal."

As I explained, Sky lay across my legs and demanded

attention. When I mentioned that the hunters might come back to Fairy Falls *again*, he growled loudly enough that I leaned back in case he turned into a monster once more.

"I haven't heard anything from the police." Nathan wisely edged away from Sky too. "Or my sister, though she might not know yet. I guess Arabella wants to keep the theft quiet."

"Yeah, but the gossiping witches are the reason word got out about the portal in the first place," I said. "I have no idea who stole it, but I've been tasked with finding the thief before the hunters step in, so I need all the help I can get."

"Miaow," Sky growled.

"Also, you aren't the only one throwing a tantrum because I wasn't fast enough to check in with you," I told Sky. "The elves think I'm snubbing them too. I'm expecting an invitation to visit their king at some point— which I ought to accept, because there's a chance one of *them* might be the thief."

Nathan's brows shot up. "Can the elves even use the portal?"

"Elves and fairies both can, but humans can't unless they have an invitation from one of the fairies on the other side of the portal," I said. "From what my dad told me, it doesn't sound as simple a matter as buying a portal from the goblin market and skipping over to the fairy realm."

"I imagine not." Nathan attempted to join me in petting Sky, who promptly pinned his legs down too. "My next shift is tomorrow morning, around the time you leave for the office. If you want to get up earlier and have a look around the lake again, we can do that."

"Good call." At least I had people willing to help me out. "My dad is talking to the other fairies, so that leaves me to question the humans. And find more witnesses." Not to mention the cabinet itself, which might contain clues of its own.

"Good." Nathan reached out and touched my arm, dodging Sky's claws in the process—apparently my cat objected to anyone being petted but him. "You shouldn't have to deal with all of this yourself."

"Story of my life." Though Nathan would be the one who had to handle the fallout if the hunters came back.

For everyone's sakes, I had to find the thief before then.

6

———

My subconscious must have expected a visit from the elf king's pixie ally, because I was already awake when a tap on the window jerked my eyes open. A shower of glitter greeted me when I tilted my head sideways to peer through the glass. I hadn't seen the pixie in a while, but like Sky, he'd probably gone into hiding after Aveline had moved into my flat.

Nathan didn't stir, so I slipped out of bed as quietly as possible and opened the window a crack.

"Who sent you?" I whispered to the pixie. "The elves' king?"

The pixie nodded then zipped through the open window and flew around the room in a circle. Glitter trailed in his wake, landing on the bed and in Nathan's hair. Oops.

"Nathan," I whispered. "The elves want to see me."

"Huh?" When the pixie fluttered down and landed on his head, Nathan's eyes opened. "What—?"

"Sorry." I stifled a laugh as he bemusedly sat up,

nudging the pixie out of his hair with a hand. "The elves sent an envoy."

He blinked sleepily. "Now? It's dawn."

"They usually come calling for me early in the morning." At least they hadn't dragged me out of work. "I need to talk to the elf king anyway."

He raised a brow. "I assume your familiar won't mind you leaving him again?"

"Hope not." I glanced at Sky, who was a fluffy lump at the end of the bed, but he didn't stir when I walked past and grabbed my clothes. I promptly dropped them when the pixie landed on Sky's head. *Uh-oh.*

"Miaow," he growled, and the pixie hastily departed to the other side of the bed.

I hurried over and crouched beside my cat. "Sky, I'm going to talk to the elf king. You can come with me if you like, since I'll probably drop by and talk to the fairies on the way back too. Nathan, do you want to meet me by the lake afterwards? I doubt the elf king will keep me for too long, and we still need to look for that cabinet."

"Sure." He yawned, swatting the pixie out of his hair again. "Sounds like a plan."

I'd have to keep an eye on the time to avoid being late for work, but at least I had a solid couple of hours to get some sleuthing in.

I shooed the pixie out of the room while I got dressed, but when I left Nathan's house, Sky was waiting outside. I hadn't seen him leave the bedroom, but that was fairy cats for you.

At least he hadn't stopped me from leaving, though I wasn't entirely sure he'd got over his huff yesterday. While the pixie zipped ahead of me down the quiet street, I snapped my fingers, and my wings unfurled behind my shoulders. Flying was much faster than walking, and before I knew it, we'd reached the forest.

When I entered, Bramble appeared so suddenly from among the bushes that I nearly jumped out of my skin. "Come with me, Blair Wilkes."

"Good morning to you too." I looked for Sky, but he'd vanished amid the trees; evidently he didn't want to come with me to see the elf king.

Bramble didn't speak a word as we followed the twisting path to the elves' territory. An uncomfortable silence lingered between the two of us despite my awkward attempts to start up conversation. I knew it had been several months since my last visit, but Bramble and I weren't exactly close friends. When we reached the foot of a steep hill, he mutely gestured towards the tunnel that led into the main part of the elves' home and indicated for me to go ahead of him.

Since the average elf was below four feet tall, I had to duck to get inside and crawl through in an undignified manner. At the end of the tunnel was a clearing in which the elf king sat upon his tree stump throne. Not much had changed since my last visit; he still wore bark-coloured clothes similar to his subjects, while his fellow elves surrounded the throne armed with the sharpened sticks that they used as weapons.

Crouched before the elf king, I ducked my head in awkward deference. Whispers flitted between the trees, and I heard my own name several times. I did my best to ignore our audience and lifted my head. "Hello, your Majesty."

"Blair Wilkes," he said. "I was beginning to wonder if you'd left Fairy Falls altogether."

"Erm. I've been busy…"

"Busy stirring things up, I hear," said the Elf King.

"With the Head Witches. They have never been friends of ours."

Oh. The witches had something of a contentious history with the elves and the fairies, and I'd forgotten he might take issue with me attending their meeting.

"My friend Rebecca is a Head Witch," I reminded him. "She doesn't want to be, since she's only eleven, but the Head Witches' rules are rigid, and I had to go to the meeting to help keep her safe. It's a good job I was there, because two of them were murdered and Rebecca herself was almost arrested—"

"I heard the rumours, Blair Wilkes," he said, cutting through my explanation. "I am not entirely ignorant of the world outside of the forest, and I was unsurprised when I heard that two Head Witches were murdered by another. What *did* surprise me was that the Knotgrass Coven still possessed a portal into the fairies' realm."

"What do you mean, *still?*" I forgot all about my contrition, my head snapping upwards. "You knew they had a portal and you didn't mention it?"

A scowl broke out on his face. "It's not my responsibility to keep you informed, Blair Wilkes. The coven's members were unable to use the portal, so I judged the matter irrelevant."

Hardly irrelevant. "She can't use it, then. Arabella, I mean."

"She believes the portal to be little more than a trinket, a curiosity."

I noted his use of the present tense. "Erm… did you know the portal was stolen yesterday?"

The Elf King rose to his feet, and tension tightened the air. "No, I certainly did not."

As the other elves stirred around him, whispering among themselves, my nerves faltered, but I forced myself to speak regardless. "It was stolen by someone in Fairy Falls. At least, that's what they think."

"Who is 'they'?"

"The witches—and the hunters." My voice wavered as the whispers attained a hostile edge, but I continued. "The witches want me to find out who took the portal so that the hunters don't come here instead. The cabinet itself was found in the lake, but it's empty."

"The witches think the fairies were responsible, don't they?" The Elf King watched me with narrowed eyes. "They certainly have reason to steal the portal back, given their links to that realm and their history with the witches."

"They wouldn't have." I decided not to point out that the elves' own history with the witches was equally tangled. "Arabella wants me to find the thief, though. You knew she had the portal—do you know who originally gave it to her family?"

"It has been with her coven for longer than either of us has been alive," he said. "Unlike the fairies, we are not ageless."

The elves' whispering continued, while it struck me that this wasn't really a great place for a private chat. The elves would never leave me alone with their king, though, so I tried to tune out their whispering and hoped none of them were preparing to stab me with their pointy sticks once I left the company of the king.

"Humans can't use the portal without an invitation from a fairy. You knew that?"

"Correct."

I debated mentioning that the elves *could* use the portal, but I didn't need to give them another reason to turn me into a Blair-shaped pincushion. "Can anyone from the other side get *out* of the portal?"

"You already know the answer to that question, Blair,"

he said. "Otherwise, nobody would have been able to take the sceptre."

He knew about that too? Upon seeing my expression, he tutted. "Do you think me entirely ignorant of recent events? My messengers talk to many people, and we know of the act of carelessness on the Head Witches' part."

My mouth parted. "My dad doesn't think it's possible for someone to have come out of the portal and taken the sceptre. The cabinet was locked."

The elf king scoffed. "A lock is no threat, given what the fairies' magic can do."

"They can't use the sceptre, can they?" That was beside the point, though, and while I was curious as to what other secrets he'd been sitting on, I was also aware that I didn't have much time before I had to go to work, and I'd been intending to search for clues near the lake with Nathan. "Do you… do you have any suspicions about who might have taken it?"

"No." He gave me a long stare that made my skin prickle. "However, I wanted to warn you to be careful with the fairies."

I blinked. "I thought you'd be more likely to warn me to be careful with the witches."

"You've already ignored that advice," he growled. "Now we all may suffer for it."

Now I remembered why I didn't make a habit of paying visits to the forest elves. Their endless sense of impending doom got old after a while. "I'll be careful. Thank you for talking to me."

He waved a hand in dismissal. Before I turned away, I risked a surreptitious look around the clearing on the off chance that the portal was hidden behind a tree or something. I didn't see any sign of a giant mirror among the muttering elves, though there was no good reason the elves would have brought what was effectively a door into enemy territory into their own home, from which anyone or anything else might emerge to attack them.

No... the thief wasn't here. I'd need to look elsewhere.

Bramble didn't deign to accompany me out of the elves' part of the forest, so I took several wrong turnings on my way back to familiar ground. As I climbed uphill, I came to an abrupt halt when I spied none other than Aveline Hollyhock meandering through the woods, making enough noise with her walking stick to cause a flock of birds to depart the nearby trees in a flurry of wings. *What's she doing in here?*

I hastily snapped my fingers and glamoured myself invisible before she saw me. Aveline's attention was focused on the bushes, gaze sweeping around as if she was looking for something. Despite my earlier suspicions, she didn't display any signs of having hidden a mirror anywhere on her person, though. Conscious of the short time I had left before I needed to get to work, I went to find the path to the fairies' clearing so I could check in with my dad before I met Nathan by the lake.

Dad answered my knock on his cottage door immediately and greeted me with a smile. "Hey, Blair."

"Hey." I closed the door behind me and followed him into the living room. "Did you manage to speak to the others yesterday?"

"Yes, I did," he said. "I told the other fairies, including Conor, about the missing portal, but he was more concerned about who might come *out* of the portal than who was responsible for stealing it. Nobody here has any idea who it was."

"The elf king said the same," I said. "He insisted on sending the pixie to wake me up at dawn so I could pay him a visit. Turns out the elves already knew the Knotgrass Coven owned a portal, but not that someone stole it."

"Interesting," he said. "Did they have any insights to give?"

"No… well, I wondered if one of them might have been responsible, but whoever took the portal can't have been worried about who might be lurking on the other side. Given how paranoid and territorial the elves can be, I don't see them taking the risk."

"Exactly," he said. "I have to admit I didn't think through all the potential ramifications when you told me of the theft, but if the court on the other side is unfriendly towards humans, the thief has potentially endangered everyone in Fairy Falls."

"If they hated humans, why would the fairies have given Arabella's coven the portal?"

"Perhaps they made an exception," he replied. "I'm speculating, but it's not unheard of for ambitious princes to forge allegiances with those they would ordinarily see as beneath them."

I thought of Rowe Clearwater, and a trickle of fear ran down my spine. "The Elf King didn't seem to think a locked cabinet door would stop a determined fairy from getting out of the portal either."

He shook his head. "Perhaps not, but we'd know if there was another fairy in the area. Conor, for one, is always on alert for potential trouble."

That would have to do. "Okay. Nathan and I are going to look around and see if the empty cabinet is still by the lake, but I just wanted to make sure none of the fairies saw or heard anything yesterday before we go looking for other clues."

"They didn't," he answered. "Remember that we can't even *see* the lake from our part of the forest, and given the current rumours, I don't blame the other fairies for not venturing far from our homes."

"Which rumours?" I frowned. "You mean the Head Witches' meeting? The elves somehow knew about that too."

He inclined his head. "It's not surprising. They have pixies and other small fairies listening out for anything that might concern them, and so do we."

My chest tightened. Even after all this time, the fairies didn't feel safe, but who could blame them? "I understand. I was just concerned at how fast the news spread. The elves even knew the sceptre was stolen from Arabella's house."

"They did?" His brows shot up. "I don't know how they would have found out. None of the fairies knew until you told me."

"Yeah… I don't get it either," I said. "Anyway, the elves' king also said that nobody is likely to know who originally gifted Arabella's coven that portal except someone who was alive back then. The elves don't live as long as the fairies do."

"True," he said. "However, it's incredibly rare for a fairy to invite a human into their realm. I might have done so for your mother, but I would have put both of us at risk in the process."

My heart gave a jolt. "She never met the rest of your family?"

His shoulders stiffened. "Blair… they might be my family by blood, but after the years we've spent apart, we're all but strangers to one another. The fairies who live there aren't anything like those who choose to live here among humans, and even if they do forgive me for my absence, they're unlikely to acknowledge a half-human child as one of their own."

Ouch. That's what I got for being overly curious about

my mysterious estranged family members. "It's fine. I have more than enough family to keep up with in this realm, let alone another one."

His tone softened. "I will never regret giving up that life for you and your mother, Blair. It was worth it."

My eyes stung. I understood how he felt, kind of—I could hardly imagine fitting back into the normal world after spending so long living in the magical one. "I'm glad."

"Try not to dwell on it," he added. "You need to go and meet Nathan, right?"

"Right." I had to squash down the part of me that wanted to ask more questions. What was the use in putting myself through that kind of misery when I had a life of my own and a thief to find?

"I'll keep my ear open for any news." He hugged me goodbye and walked me to the door.

As I left the cottage, Ani came running into the clearing, her eyes wide and her hair dishevelled as if she'd flown across the lake without stopping.

"Blair," she said. "You—your boyfriend is out there. I saw him on the way in."

"Oh, good." Then I took stock of her shaken appearance. "What's wrong?"

"Blair… did you know the hunters were near the lake?"

"No." Oh no. They'd already come to Fairy Falls? Maybe Arabella had lost patience, though she hadn't even given me a full day to find the thief. "They shouldn't be here."

I should have known they wouldn't stay away for long.

7

———

I flew out of the fairies' part of the woods and didn't stop until I reached the lake's edge. There, I found Nathan arguing with Erin, his younger sister. The two shared the same dark hair, though Erin's was longer. She wore a tank top that showed off her muscular shoulders.

"Absolutely not," Nathan was saying to her. "We talked about this, Erin."

Nearby, Erin's fiancé, Buck, caught my eye, which abruptly reminded me that I still had my fairy wings out. As another ex-hunter and one of the few other half-fairies I'd met, he kept his own wings hidden, though his long blond hair and striking blue eyes hinted at his fairy origins.

"Guys, stop arguing," Buck told the others. "Blair's here."

"What's going on?" I snapped my fingers, and my wings vanished. "Are the hunters here? One of the fairies told me they were."

"No—not inside Fairy Falls, at any rate," Nathan answered. "They're on the other side of the border. Erin wants to confront them, but we'd be inviting unnecessary conflict."

"Unnecessary?" said Erin. "The fairies already know the hunters are there, right? They feel threatened, I bet, and those intruders aren't going to voluntarily leave by themselves."

"I think we should talk to them," I ventured. "If we're going to look around the lake where the cabinet showed up, they're likely to spot us anyway."

Nathan grimaced. "That's what I'm afraid of. I know you need to find out who took Arabella's portal, but if the hunters are doing the same, they'll never let us step in."

"Why'd she volunteer you to help her, Blair?" Erin wanted to know.

"Luck of the draw," I quipped. "Actually, I have no idea why Arabella decided that I'm the person for the job, but since the other option is to let the hunters take over, I don't really have a choice. She gave me three days."

"Then she sent the hunters in anyway?" Erin paced along the shore, peering over the lake. "Shifty."

"They might not be here on her orders." Nathan strode behind his sister. "We can't discount the possibility of the hunters choosing to get involved of their own accord. The theft of a fairy portal is bound to be of interest."

"That's right." Erin swivelled to face me. "Nathan told me some of it, but I'd like to hear the story from you."

"We can talk on the way," Nathan told her. "If you really want to talk to the hunters, Blair."

"I wouldn't say I *want* to talk to them." The hunters and I invariably clashed whenever we met, and their near arrest of Rebecca had made me even less inclined to want to play nice with them. "I want to make sure they're not planning to come and harass the fairies, though."

That would depend on *which* hunters were present. The Inquisitor's former allies were no fans of the fairies, but Linda Graham wasn't someone I'd trust around them either. Her team had come close to arresting Rebecca and had nearly led to Meredith stealing the portal with her own hands.

I filled Erin and Buck in on the events of the past couple of weeks as we walked around the lake's edge until we reached the border of Fairy Falls, where rolling hills covered the lake's right flank. My heart gave a lurch when I spotted three figures standing near a sodden heap of wood that might have once been a cabinet.

"Why'd they drop the cabinet in the lake?" Erin peered at the wooden pile. "Isn't it less conspicuous than a portal into the fairy realm?"

"The portal looks like a giant mirror, which makes it easier to hide." Nathan glanced over at me. "The cabinet was locked initially, right, Blair?"

"I thought so." I squinted at the distant figures, my pulse skittering. Something about the trio seemed awfully familiar to me. "Do any of you recognise them?"

Erin's eyes widened. "Yeah… I know those guys."

The closer we drew to the trio, the more certain I felt of their identities, though I didn't know their real names. I'd nicknamed those particular hunters Sleepy, Dopey, and Grumpy the last time I'd encountered them—which had been months ago, before they'd been demoted.

Why, then, were they back in Fairy Falls?

My steps slowed as we neared the three men. As far as the hunters went, the three were amateurs. Sleepy, tall and thin, typically looked as if he needed a nap. Dopey, shorter and broader, wore a bemused expression as if he'd been dropped off by a UFO with no recollection of how he got here. Grumpy, whose bald patch was distinctly sunburned, glared at the sun as if he wanted to punch it out of the sky.

"What are you doing?" Erin called to their group. "If you get too close to the lake, something might come out and eat you."

"You." Dopey's gaze slid across our group. "I know you."

"That's Blair Wilkes." Grumpy turned his glower on me instead. "The reason we got demoted."

"What are you doing out here?" I studied the ruined cabinet, which resembled little more than a sodden pile of wood lying in the shallows of the lake. "Do you know what that is?"

"A cabinet," said Dopey. "From—"

Grumpy elbowed him in the chest. "Don't tell her anything, fool. She already nearly cost us our jobs."

"The hunters kept you on staff?" Nathan strode out to meet them. "Who sent you here?"

"You're not one of us." Sleepy yawned. "We don't have to tell you anything."

"Unless your guilty conscience brought you back to the scene of the crime," Grumpy added. "Stolen anything lately, Blair?"

"You think I'm the thief?" I stifled a laugh. "Arabella Knotgrass hired *me*, not the hunters."

Dopey blinked a couple of times. "Who's Arabella?"

Grumpy gave him another elbow to the ribs. "She's the one who owned *this*, and she's going to get us our positions back. Now, be quiet."

"Oh." Comprehension dawned on me. "You think you can regain your lost glory if you find the thief, is that it?"

"Watch it, you," said Grumpy. "You already ruined our reputations. I won't let you do it again."

"No, you're already doing a spectacular job on your

own," said Erin, with a snort. "Maybe the thief's lying at the bottom of the lake. Why not look for yourselves?"

Dopey moved towards the water, and Grumpy reached out a hand and grabbed him by the scruff of his neck. "Ignore her, fool."

"The portal itself might be in the lake," I ventured. "I can't promise the merpeople will be happy if you go for a swim on their territory, but you don't have permission to enter Fairy Falls either."

"Exactly," said Nathan. "Whether you're here on behalf of the hunters or not, I'm Fairy Falls's head of security and the person who'll have to deal with the consequences of any trouble you cause."

"*She's* the troublemaker." Sleepy indicated me. "Besides, we're not in your town, so you can't throw us out."

"Then you can go away by yourselves," Erin told him. "Blair is the one who's been asked to look into the theft of the portal."

Dopey grunted. "We got here first."

"You're not doing anything but standing around." They might not be here for official reasons, but I refused point-blank to go into fairy mode in front of an audience of the Inquisitor's former allies.

"Who exactly *are* you answering to?" Nathan asked. "If I give your supervisors a call, will they back you up?"

"Please do," Erin added. "It'll be fun."

Grumpy's face turned brick red. "What's it to you?"

"You have a history of harassing the town's citizens," Nathan said. "We're the security team, and we've been sent to investigate that cabinet. Go on, leave."

When the trio didn't budge, Nathan, Erin, and Buck advanced on them. We outnumbered them, at least if you counted me, though whenever I used magic in a crisis, I tended to accidentally make it rain glitter. Regardless, I could see the hesitation on the three hunters' faces as they weighed the odds.

Grumpy made up the others' minds for them. "We'll come back later."

"Good riddance," Erin said in an audible whisper while the three hunters sloped away from the lakeside. "I bet nobody gave them orders to come here. They wanted to prove themselves and get back into the hunters' good graces."

"Maybe," I said, "but don't forget who they used to work with. They might have less than five brain cells among them, but they have a knack for picking dangerous allies."

Like Mrs Dailey… and the Inquisitor. The latter had been on my mind more recently, though Blythe had told me at the meeting that her mother had been scheming from her jail cell, trying to use blackmail to convince the other local witches to make alliances with her. Might those three troublemakers have interacted with her recently too? They shouldn't have been allowed to stay in this region after their former screwups, but it wouldn't surprise me if they'd been overlooked by the hunters' management in the chaos that had ensued after their leader had been unmasked as a fairy. Quite understandably, the supervisors' attention had been elsewhere.

When I was sure the three hunters were a safe distance away, I snapped my fingers and turned into my fairy mode to look at the cabinet's remains.

"See anything?" Erin squinted at the cabinet. "Looks like a pile of wood to me. Unless you actually think the portal is in the lake?"

"I don't think so, but someone desperately wanted to get it out of the cabinet without using a key." There was nothing of the cabinet's doors left. "Looks like they blew it up."

"I wonder how those three hunters found out?" Erin remarked. "They don't work for the same branch as the ones Arabella hired, right?"

"They don't," I confirmed, "but I bet they've had their ears open for any opportunities to boost their reputations. Especially ones that involve screwing over Fairy Falls."

Is Mrs Dailey involved, though? She would have leapt at the chance to get her hands on a portal to Fairyland, surely. The portal would give her a way out of jail *and* a chance to get back in touch with her buddy, the Inquisitor. Of course, I didn't know if even her considerable magical skills would help her survive in a realm as hostile to humans as the fairy world was supposed to be, but I wouldn't put anything past her.

"I won't allow them to come back." Nathan watched the hunters' retreating figures cross the hillside. "I'll tell Steve they were here, for all the good that'll do. Did your dad have any updates, Blair?"

I shook my head. "None of the fairies saw anything weird by the lake yesterday, but I did see Aveline Hollyhock wandering around the woods earlier."

"Aveline?" Erin echoed. "The Head Witch?"

"Former Head Witch," I amended. "Rebecca's new tutor. I have to admit part of me wants *her* to be the one who took the portal, so I have an excuse to kick her out of my flat."

Erin snorted. "It's ridiculous that being a former Head Witch means she gets away with that."

"I know, but Madame Grey wants her to tutor Rebecca," I said. "Aveline misses carrying a sceptre, though, so I did wonder if she might have considered the one on the other side of the portal."

"Was the sceptre stolen by a fairy?" asked Buck. "Weird. I wouldn't think they'd be able to use it."

"My dad doesn't think the sceptre is in the fairies' realm," I said. "But I couldn't help wondering if the thief wanted that sceptre as well as the portal itself."

"A witch stole it?" Erin scrunched up her forehead. "That checks out. The covens have lived in the area for generations and have a long tradition of backstabbing, so it makes more sense for a witch to be the thief than a fairy."

"Exactly." I was glad someone else supported my theory. "I wanted to find out who gave the portal to Arabella's coven in the first place, but while the fairies live a lot longer than the rest of us do, none of the ones in Fairy Falls were around back then."

"Would the vampires know?" Erin suggested.

"You might be onto something there. I'll ask Vincent after work." Speaking of which, I hadn't checked the time since before I'd gone into the forest. Oops. "Also, I'm pretty sure I'm late."

"You'd better go," Nathan said. "I'll keep watch for those hunters, okay?"

I hugged him goodbye. "Can you let me know if they come back?"

"Of course," he replied. "I'll text you if there are any new updates. I'll tell Steve, too, but since the hunters didn't actually trespass over the border, he might not be willing to take any action."

"He wouldn't if they *did* trespass," added Erin. "I'll see you later. Good luck, Blair."

Leaving the others by the lake, I flew to work in fairy mode to save on time. Skidding to a halt in front of the office, I zipped into the reception area to a startled Callie.

She jumped to her feet and then sat down again. "Oh —sorry, Blair, I didn't recognise you for a second there."

"Sorry." Flustered, I snapped my fingers and replaced my human glamour, wondering if I'd ever get used to remembering to switch between the two in appropriate settings. At least my boss hadn't seen me as a fairy, though she might be more annoyed at my lateness than my wings and the glitter I'd dropped all over the reception area.

While the others were sympathetic to my recent distractions despite not knowing the specifics, I remained on edge, expecting Veronica to come in to reprimand me for showing up late or Madame Grey to give her another call with bad news. I'd forgotten to ask Nathan to pass on the news of the Inquisitor's old allies showing up, and if Steve didn't tell her, I'd have to drop by the witches' head-quarters on my way home from work.

The Inquisitor didn't send them here… did he? Surely not.

That thought naturally led me down a rabbit hole of imagining what the Inquisitor was doing at the moment, which was somewhat difficult when I didn't know what the fairy realm *looked* like. My only point of comparison was the goblin market that had come to town months ago and had woven a spell that had ensnared my foster parents, but I shoved the memory away. If the Inquisitor had been involved with the portal's theft, wouldn't he have left a clue? He might be wary of drawing too much attention, since he wasn't in a position of power among the hunters any longer, but I couldn't imagine he'd been doing nothing but hiding in a cave for the past six or more months since our last encounter.

Somehow, I made it to the end of the workday. Nathan hadn't messaged me, so I assumed the hunters had had more sense than to come back. As planned, I headed for the witches' headquarters after work. I had a magic lesson, which I was not remotely prepared for, but since I remained at a dead end in my investigation into the theft of the portal, perhaps a magical duelling session with Rebecca would help me shake some ideas loose.

I found Blythe and her sister talking outside the building. The former stopped midsentence when she saw me approaching and said, "I'll see you later, Rebecca."

"Blythe," I called after her. "Can I talk to you?"

"No," she replied. "If you want me to help you hunt for thieves, you can forget it. I don't know the fairies."

"Did you know the hunters were hanging around the lake earlier, then?" I couldn't figure out what her problem was this time. "Do you remember Sleepy, Dopey, and Grumpy?"

She blinked. "Who?"

Rebecca looked equally confused. "Those aren't their real names, are they?"

"No, but they worked with—" I broke off, unwilling to say her name. "With she-who-must-not-be-named. They're inept at their jobs, but they seem to be trying to win their bosses' favour back by finding the thief."

The colour drained from Rebecca's face as she realised who I meant, but Blythe remained impassive. "Don't bother my sister with that nonsense, Blair. Talk to your boyfriend instead. He's supposed to be in charge of the town's security, isn't he?"

She walked off without giving me the chance to answer.

Rebecca lifted her head, gripping her sceptre in both hands. "The hunters came back?"

"Nathan sent them packing, which I would have told your sister if she'd stuck around." I watched her retreat. "Has she got it into her head that what happened at the meeting was my fault?"

Blythe and I had never been friends, though we'd been forced into a reluctant truce when Rebecca had been accused of murder, and as a result, I'd thought we still shared a common purpose. Apparently Blythe disagreed.

Rebecca's gaze dropped. "You know she doesn't like talking about *her*."

"Yeah, but you'd think she'd want to know her former minions were sniffing around the lake."

"You know how overprotective of me she's been since the meeting," Rebecca said. "She'll get over it."

"I hope so." If we found ourselves facing a common enemy soon enough, I needed all the allies I could get. "How're lessons going with Aveline, anyway?"

"All right," she replied. "She likes to teach me in the forest for some reason. Says it helps her think more clearly."

"The forest?" Maybe that was why I'd seen her wandering around earlier. I remained sceptical that she was entirely focused on Rebecca's education as Head Witch, but *she* certainly hadn't brought the hunters here.

"Yeah." Rebecca took a startled step back when the doors to the witches' headquarters flew open and Madame Grey came striding out, her cloak streaming behind her.

"Madame Grey?" I jumped out of her way to avoid being knocked aside by her determined march. "Where are you going?"

"Arabella's house." She pulled out her wand. "She's been attacked."

8

———

As the door swung closed behind Madame Grey, I stared at her. "What's going on? Who attacked Arabella?"

The attack must have been serious if it had rattled Madame Grey of all people, but I hadn't known Arabella was in the habit of calling her fellow coven leaders to ask for advice.

"I don't know, Blair," she replied, "but Arabella claims it was a fairy."

"A fairy?" *Oh. Oh no.* "From—from inside the portal?"

How? If the portal is here in Fairy Falls, that's not possible. Is it?

Rebecca paled. "No way."

"I don't have all the details," said Madame Grey, "but I intend to talk to the town's security team before I go to Arabella herself. If the attacker *did* come out of the portal, someone might have seen them."

I hurried behind her as she swept away from the witches' headquarters. "I can text Nathan and ask if he saw anything. He was already keeping an eye on the border, since those three hunters showed up earlier—did you know?"

"No, I didn't." She halted midstride and swung towards me with enough intensity to make me want to back slowly away. "Which hunters?"

"A certain trio who were supposed to be demoted." I grimaced. "I called them Sleepy, Dopey, and Grumpy. Remember who they worked with?"

Her eyes narrowed. "Right… let's see what Steve has to say, then."

I blinked, surprised that the police station would be her first stop of choice. "Ah… Madame Grey, do you think Steve would be of any help in this situation? Arabella isn't local, and he's not officially looking for the thief anyway."

"You are." Blythe, who evidently hadn't walked as far away as I'd thought, backed into view. "Who attacked Arabella?"

"A fairy," I told her. "Possibly from behind that missing portal."

Blythe went as deathly pale as her sister had at the mention of her mother. "No. That's impossible."

"It isn't. Unfortunately." Blythe might have no love for the local fairies, but the possibility of an attacker having come from somewhere within Fairy Falls itself would freak anyone out.

"It's certainly possible." Madame Grey continued to march onwards down the street. "After the attack, Arabella now has more incentive to contact the hunters, which would certainly be of interest to Steve even if the attack itself does not concern him."

My heart lurched. If she was right, Arabella wouldn't hire the three buffoons we'd met by the lake. No, she'd go to Linda Graham or someone similar—someone ruthless and uncompromising and uncaring of how many lives she upended in her pursuit of justice.

"I wish I knew where that portal was." My hands clenched at my sides. "The fairies definitely don't have it, and I don't think the elves do either. If the person who attacked Arabella didn't come from inside the portal itself, they might have nothing to do with the thief at all."

Madame Grey turned back to me, the sunlight reflecting on her glasses and amplifying her stern expression. "That may well be true, but Arabella saw nothing of her attacker. She believes they were glamoured, like the thief, which is a potential connection she will not overlook."

Blythe coughed. "Not all the fairies are your friends, Blair."

"I'm aware of that," I said testily. "I faced off against Inquisitor Hare, remember?"

Rebecca flinched. "It's not *him*, is it? If his allies were hanging around…"

"What exactly were those three hunters doing?" Madame Grey asked me.

"Hanging around, staring at the empty cabinet," I replied. "I figured they wanted to regain their lost glory by catching the thief."

"Hardly worth bothering with," said Blythe. "They're hopeless."

"Unless *they* stole the portal," Rebecca said. "Isn't that the sort of thing they'd do? They want their reputations back, so they might have stolen the portal to frame the fairies *and* make themselves into heroes."

Her idea held merit, but I had a hard time imagining those three hunters smuggling the portal out of Arabella's house without magic. "I think they're too incompetent to be the thieves."

"That's enough speculation." Madame Grey pinched the bridge of her nose. "Rebecca, Blythe, you don't need to concern yourselves with this. Blair…"

"Arabella hired me," I reminded her. "Even if she changes her mind, I owe it to the fairies to find the real culprit. Especially if a fairy *attacked* her. I know it wasn't one of ours, but I bet word has spread about her having that portal, so the person who attacked her might have been wanting to steal it too."

"Didn't I say that's enough theories?" Madame Grey slowed her pace as we neared the police station. "You might be correct, Blair, but she wants a person to point the finger of blame at, and our local fairies are the most natural target."

No kidding. "A fairy might have attacked her, but far more witches know the layout of the Knotgrass Coven's house. With magic, they would have easily been able to hide themselves and levitate the cabinet out of the window. I still think the thief came from the covens."

"If they were stealthy, why'd they drop the cabinet in the lake?" Blythe scoffed. "I suppose if they were as incompetent at transportation spells as you are…"

"That's quite enough, Blythe," said Madame Grey as heat flooded my face. "You and Rebecca should go home. I'm sure Rita will be willing to let you skip today's lesson. You, too, Blair… Unless you'd like to talk to Steve too?"

I'd sooner ride a broomstick with Dopey. "Not really, but I have a limited amount of time to find evidence for Arabella, and that's assuming she'll be patient enough to wait. I can't just go home and forget this."

"I'll call Veronica and ask her to give you tomorrow off work," she said. "I think she'll be willing, given the circumstances."

"Oh, thanks." I'd much sooner be inside the office

dealing with problem clients than talking to an angry coven leader who was convinced that a fairy had tried to have her assassinated, but Arabella's dilemma had to take priority if I wanted to keep the hunters out of Fairy Falls. "I'll see you later, Rebecca."

As Blythe and Rebecca walked away, Madame Grey studied my face for a moment. "When you first came to Fairy Falls, Blair…"

"Oh?" I tensed, braced for a reminder of how much upheaval I'd caused in Fairy Falls over the years. While Madame Grey had stood behind me from the start, it felt as if recently the universe was determined to prove that people like Steve and Arabella were right—that I was a force of utter chaos who'd brought nothing but trouble in the time I'd lived here.

"When you first came to Fairy Falls," Madame Grey repeated, "I had an instinct you would bring change, but I didn't foresee how far afield the impact of your arrival would spread."

"You didn't think I'd indirectly cause the downfall of the Head Witches?" I said wryly.

"The Head Witches have been in dire need of a shift in perspective for a long time," she said. "I suspect Arabella's attitude towards you is due to bitterness at her own world-view being shifted. Regardless, I have faith in you."

My face warmed, though a knot remained in my chest. "I'm trying my best, but I can't guarantee that I'll figure it out before Arabella loses patience with me and sends in the hunters. Then the fairies… They'll never trust me again."

"You aren't responsible for Arabella's choices," she said. "If she hadn't kept that portal in her house after the incident with the sceptre, this situation might have been avoided."

I blinked. "You expected someone to attack her?"

She inclined her head. "Arabella must have known that word of the portal's existence would spread outside of the group of people who attended the meeting. I suspect that the person who attacked her didn't realise it was already gone."

I thought she told me to stop speculating. "How'd she escape the attack, do you know?"

"Her house has security spells on it," said Madame Grey. "I need to talk to her again to learn the specifics, but she thinks her assailant escaped out of a window, like the thief did."

"I guess I don't blame her for assuming they were the same person." I dropped my gaze. "I don't know who took the portal, though, and I'm out of ideas for people to question."

"Talk to my granddaughter. She might have some ideas." She turned back towards the police station. "In the meantime, I have to talk to the police. I can ask if they're keeping an eye out for those three hunters while I'm there."

"I should have told you right away," I blurted. "I was running late for work at the time. The hunters had already left, but Nathan said he'd message me if they came back—"

She held up a hand to silence me. "I understand, Blair. I doubt those three hunters stole the portal or attacked Arabella, so they aren't my priority."

"I know they're not the sharpest tools, but they were Mrs Dailey's allies *and* worked with the Inquisitor," I said. "What if they have more competent allies?"

"That," she said, "is not outside of the realm of possibility."

A chill arced down my spine. "Do you think he still has influence over the hunters?"

"That, I cannot say," she said. "However, I have little doubt he's aware of the portal's existence now, even if he wasn't before."

The anxious pit in my stomach grew. "Do *you* know who gave that portal to Arabella's coven in the first place? I know it's an heirloom, but it seems strange for the fairies to have entrusted humans with a way into their realm."

"Yes… Arabella has stayed close-lipped on the subject," she said. "Out of shame, perhaps, that one of her predecessors was allied with the fairies."

I swallowed. "I wondered if the person who originally gifted the portal to her coven might have stolen it back… But it's not someone in Fairy Falls."

Movement stirred behind the automatic doors to the police station, catching Madame Grey's attention. "I'll contact you tomorrow, Blair. Talk to your friends and get some rest. It'll help."

All right. I certainly didn't want a chat with Steve, while Arabella was bound to be even less pleasant than usual after the attempt on her life. I trusted Madame Grey to handle them both.

As I walked away from the police station, I messaged both Nathan and Alissa, hoping one of them would help me figure out a direction. I didn't want to go home without making another effort to gather clues pointing to the portal's thief—or Arabella's attacker, if they turned out to be the same person—so I found myself wandering back towards the forest.

Inside, I spotted a familiar figure clambering over the tree roots. *Aveline.* I slowed my pace as I watched her meander down the forest path, before my curiosity got the better of me and I approached her.

Upon noticing me, Aveline grunted. "You again?"

"I could say the same to you." I followed her gaze to

the thick trees ahead of us. "What're you looking for?"

"None of your concern," she replied. "Maybe I got bored of that stuffy guest room and wanted some fresh air."

"It's *my* flat." Annoyance flared inside me. I should have known that talking to her would do nothing to improve my temper. "In case you've forgotten."

When I turned away, she laughed under her breath. "Going to find your friend? I wouldn't bother. She went into work to take over someone else's shift, in her usual ridiculous self-sacrificing manner."

"I guess you're not familiar with the concept of helping other people." I should probably watch my tongue, but the attack on Arabella and the freaked-out expression on Madame Grey's face earlier had spooked me enough that Aveline seemed tame by comparison.

"Oh, I'm familiar with the subject, but most people have no appreciation for healers. Look at that ridiculous elf."

"Thistle?" Was he back in the hospital again? I hadn't seen him near the lake earlier, but he was an expert at finding new ways to get into trouble.

"I haven't a clue," she said. "They're all the same to me."

"I wouldn't say that when you're right next to the elves' territory." Especially if Bramble was lurking in the bushes again. "I can't promise anyone will come to your defence if you get into a fight with the elves."

Aveline gave a low chuckle. "Then I'll have to give them another reminder to choose their battles wisely."

"What?" I turned back to her, momentarily forgetting my intention to leave. "What do you mean by 'another reminder'? Have you met the elves before?"

Bramble certainly knew who she was, given his

complaints about her disturbing the forest, but I hadn't known they were personally acquainted.

"Of course I have." Another laugh. "They've always been uppity little creatures who think they deserve to be exempt from the rules."

"What rules? They have as much of a right to live here as the rest of us do." My confusion turned back to annoyance. "The covens are hardly faultless, and neither are the Head Witches, for that matter. They make mistakes all the time. Look at Arabella Knotgrass."

This time she positively cackled. "Oh, I'm *not* surprised someone finally decided to put her in her place."

"You know she was attacked?"

Her laughter echoed amid the trees. "Yes, your Madame Grey really needs to be more careful to watch for eavesdroppers."

"You were spying on us." I couldn't believe she had the nerve to speak like that about Madame Grey, too, and I was half-tempted to march to the police station and tell her myself.

"Don't take it so personally," she said. "I expect Arabella will have told half the country by the week's end."

I folded my arms over my chest. "What do you think, then? Do you know who attacked her?"

"Oh, I hardly care," she said. "It's none of my business."

"It'll be all our business if she does as she threatened and sends the hunters here to question everyone—which you'll also know about, if you listened to our entire discussion." I scowled. "I thought you were here to *stop* Rebecca getting into trouble for crimes she never committed."

"Yes, which is why you shouldn't get it into your head that I'm here to help *you*, Blair Wilkes."

"No danger of that happening," I muttered. "Rebecca

has made it clear that she doesn't want to stay Head Witch, hasn't she? What does she need to learn from you?"

"Unlike you, Rebecca has accepted what she can't control," said Aveline. "You should do the same."

Wait. Does that mean she wants to stay Head Witch after all? I'd have to ask Rebecca herself, assuming Blythe ever let her sister stray from her watchful gaze. Aveline had no intention of cooperating, and this time when I walked away, she didn't call after me.

Despite knowing Alissa would be run off her feet, I went to the hospital, intending to see if Thistle was there. When I stepped through the doors, a wall of noise hit me. It took several muddled seconds for me to parse through the mixture of raised voices and the sort of obnoxious music you heard in nightclubs when everyone was too drunk to care that their eardrums were suffering.

The source came from the waiting room, where Alissa and one of the other staff members were attempting to negotiate with Thistle. The elf stood on a chair in the waiting room holding up a portable speaker that ran on magic and not electricity, and which blasted music that made the very walls of the room vibrate.

"Thistle, get down from there," Alissa was saying in exasperated tones. "Ah—hey, Blair. This isn't a good time."

"I gathered." I crossed the room to Alissa's side, hands over my ears. "How'd he end up in here? Is he injured?"

"He slept in the lake last night and gave himself a chill. As you can see, he's made a remarkable recovery."

"Typical." I had to raise my own voice to be heard over the racket. "I thought he had a girlfriend and didn't get up to this kind of nonsense anymore."

"So did I, but old habits die hard." She shuffled away from the elf's chair. "I thought you had a magic lesson today."

"Cancelled," I said, in as quiet a voice as I could manage considering the noise in the background. "Arabella was attacked, possibly by a fairy, and I'm out of ideas about who might be the thief."

"What?" She swore under her breath. "Seriously?"

"Yep." I thought back to the forest and my lingering suspicions about our unwanted house guest. "Was Aveline at home at the time, do you know?"

"No, thank the goddess. I was catching up on sleep."

Aveline wasn't there. I didn't *think* she'd have attacked Arabella, but her weird behaviour in the forest bugged me like an itch I couldn't scratch.

"Hello, Briar!" shouted a voice that rivalled the speakers for volume. Old Ava came ambling out of one of the nearby corridors and gave me a cheery wave.

"Erm… hi, Ava." After a year, I'd given up telling her "Briar" wasn't my name. Ava, who resided in one of the hospital's wards for long-term residents who'd suffered permanent spell damage, wore her usual wild-eyed expression, her hair a purple tangle and her wand's plastic replacement sticking out from behind her ear.

"Ava, go back to your room," Alissa said sternly.

"I thought there was a party."

"Not on my watch." Alissa approached the elf's chair again. "Thistle—put that thing down."

The elf responded by turning the volume up instead. I hastened for the door before I lost all hearing in both ears, but even amid the clamour of the music, I heard Ava shouting at my back.

I couldn't entirely make out the words, but I was positive I heard my name and the phrase "the winged one."

There was only one person she'd called by that title before.

9

———————

As I walked away from the hospital, I told myself I'd misheard Ava's words amid the general racket, but part of me remained unconvinced. The last time she'd used the phrase "the winged one," she'd meant *him*.

Rowe Clearwater. Inquisitor Hare.

Ava couldn't possibly know what the former Inquisitor was up to, but it wouldn't have been the first time she'd shown surprising perceptiveness. Even the name she'd used —Briar Wildflower—had been the one my mother had originally intended to give me, and when I added her warning on top of my conversation with Madame Grey earlier, I was officially rattled.

Nathan had replied to my message, so I went to meet him outside the police station. While I opted not to share my suspicions concerning the Inquisitor, the thoughts remained in the back of my mind throughout the evening. Nathan and I went on a double date at the pub that evening with Erin and Buck, where the four of us tried to come up with any new theories on who might have stolen the portal.

While Erin was full of questions about the Head Witch meeting and the portal, she and Buck knew little of the witches and weren't exactly plugged into what was going on with the hunters recently either. Erin maintained her belief that the hunters had swiped the portal and planted it here to blame the theft on the fairies, but Nathan and Buck disagreed, believing the thief was more likely to be linked to the witches instead. I thought the same, but the attack on Arabella had changed the playing field. I had a hard time believing her attacker had come *out* of the portal, and the others agreed—but what if the thief and the attacker were one and the same?

I'd need to talk to Arabella to get the full story, but it was anyone's guess as to whether she was taking visitors. I had the next day off work, but without a plan, I was at something of a loose end. Nathan suggested I sleep on it, while Sky contributed by curling up next to my head and purring all night. At least he'd got over his sulk.

When I woke up the following morning, Nathan was out patrolling, but I found a message on my phone from Alissa, asking if I wanted to grab coffee later that morning. I figured her grandmother had told her I had the day off, which I was admittedly supposed to use to find the thief, but the night hadn't brought any new revelations, and I assumed Arabella had zero desire to see me again.

After I'd showered and dressed, I went downstairs, pursued by an unusually clingy Sky.

"Miaow." He rubbed against the back of my legs, purring.

"I'm glad you've cheered up." I scratched him behind the ears with one hand. "Do you fancy helping me hunt for a thief?"

"Miaow." He lifted his head, ears pricked. Then he bounded ahead of me into the hallway, planted his paws on the shoe rack, and knocked my boots onto the floor.

"You want to go out?" I picked up one of my Seven-Millimetre Boots, which enabled me to levitate without needing to get out my wings, and tugged it onto my foot.

"Miaow." Sky reached out a paw and pushed against the door.

"Wait." I hopped on one foot, one hand on the wall to avoid losing my balance. "What's the rush?"

Hang on. He and the other fairy cats had some means of communication that didn't involve the rest of us, so it was possible he'd received a message from someone. Like — "Wait. Sky, have you seen or talked to Vincent recently?"

"Miaow." He barely waited for me to open the front door before he bounded outside, and then he beckoned to me with his tail.

"Is that where you want to go?" The vampires typically went to bed around dawn, but I'd forgotten Vincent might know about Arabella's coven's history with the fairies.

Confusingly, though, Sky walked straight past the vampires' home near the cemetery and went downhill towards the high street instead. He didn't slow until he reached the witches' headquarters, and I watched in confusion as Madame Grey emerged from the front door.

She looked unsurprised to see me. "Blair, I wondered if you might show up. I'm just going to talk to Arabella."

"You are?" I glanced down at Sky. "My cat led me here. I thought he might have picked up on something from the other fairy cats… or Vincent."

"I did meet with the vampires earlier." Madame Grey eyed him with interest. "He's a very perceptive animal. Do you want to bring him with you?"

"You want *me* to talk to Arabella? I don't have an update for her yet." If she thought I wasn't pulling my weight, she might snap and call the hunters. Assuming she hadn't already.

Hmm. Maybe I'll take Sleepy, Dopey, and Grumpy to meet her. Anyone would lose all interest in working with the hunters after meeting those three specimens, wouldn't they?

"No, but you haven't looked around the scene of the attack." Madame Grey gave me a searching gaze. "You remember what I said yesterday, don't you? Arabella's attitude towards the fairies is no reflection on you."

I squashed down the protest that rose on my tongue. I might not have seen any signs of the fairies in the room that had contained the stolen cabinet, but this was different. The thief might not have been a fairy, while the attacker almost certainly was. *Also, I didn't have Sky with me last time. He can help.*

"True." I reached for my wand. "We're going the same way as before?"

"Yes." She pulled out her own wand and raised it in front of her face. "Your cat doesn't like transportation spells, does he?"

"No, he doesn't, but he can walk on foot." I crouched beside Sky. "You still want to come with me, right?"

"Miaow."

I assumed that meant "yes." Wishing *I* had a psychic link with him, I straightened and prepared to follow Madame Grey's lead.

We waved our wands and vanished. Once again, we landed on the sloping hillside in front of the Knotgrass Coven's base, where Madame Grey gave me an approving look. "You're getting good at that spell, Blair."

I flushed at her praise. "It's easier if it's somewhere I've already been."

Somehow, Sky was already here, waiting at the foot of the hill. He watched our approach and yawned, as if he thought we were slow. Hoping that Arabella didn't object to me bringing him inside, I beckoned him to follow us to the Knotgrass Coven's house.

Behind the gate, Arabella appeared as a forbidding figure dressed in black, as if she was on her way to a funeral. "Madame Grey. I don't remember asking you to bring the fairy-witch with you too."

My heart dropped, and Sky twined himself around my legs, nudging me along. After Arabella had verified that we weren't assassins in disguise, I followed Madame Grey into the garden.

The entire place had transformed since our last visit. The bright flower beds and statues were gone, and in their place was a maze of twisting hedges that gave the impression of the walls of a fortress.

When we reached the doorstep, Arabella's gaze landed on Sky. "What's that animal?"

"My familiar," I told her. "Sky is good at sniffing out threats, and he can see things I can't, so I thought he might be able to help."

Her mouth pursed. "I assume you came here because you brought a promising update on the theft."

"Erm…" I faltered when she pulled out her wand, but she pointed it at the front door instead of at me. The click of padlocks unlocking filled the air. She'd upped her security since the attack. "I came here to look around the site of the attack to see if I could find any clues."

"I have my doubts." She pushed open the door to reveal an entrance hall that had been transformed as much as the garden had. All the mirrors and revolving doors had vanished, the space having shrunk to a narrow hallway with a single door on our right and an equally narrow staircase ahead of us. I wondered what her fellow coven members thought about her choice to make most of the rooms disappear. There didn't seem to be anyone else around, so maybe she'd kicked them out.

The sole office upstairs was as warm as a greenhouse and full of the usual coven leader paraphernalia—cabinets overflowing with files, bookcases, and a desk covered in paperwork.

"You were in here when you got attacked?" I asked. "With magic, right? But you didn't see your attacker?"

Arabella pointed at the swivel chair behind the desk. "I was sitting there when the door opened and someone on the other side cast a spell. It looked like a blast of glittering purple light, but very luckily, I have a defensive charm on my office which prevented the spell from doing more than knocking me out of my seat."

Glitter. Not good. I made out a few singe marks on the desk, and the smell of burning lingered in the air, but no glitter remained. Not that my human eyes showed the whole picture. "Weren't your fellow coven members in the building at the time?"

"What kind of an absurd question is that?" she said. "Yes, they were, but evidently the attacker concealed themselves beneath glamour. I didn't see anyone outside the room, but the spell didn't cast itself, did it?"

"Then how did they get into the actual building?" One would have thought she'd have upped her security after the portal's theft, but her desire for aesthetics might have won out over personal safety.

She whipped around with a glare. "I assume they got in through a window again, and believe me, I intend to keep them closed from now on."

No wonder it was so stiflingly hot inside her office. "And the attacker escaped via the same route?"

"That was implied. What is your cat doing?"

I glanced at Sky, who was sniffing around the desk. "Looking for clues. He's good at that."

"It's not enough." Her tone dripped with disdain. "I gave you a fair chance, Blair, but I'm no longer in need of your help."

"What—you're firing me?" She'd never hired me to begin with, of course, but she'd barely given me a day to find the thief.

"I'm dismissing you, yes." She turned to Madame Grey. "You too. I need someone willing to use force to find this assassin."

My throat went dry. "You're not going to contact the hunters? They're even less equipped to deal with fairies than the witches are."

"Incorrect," she said. "They might have been ill-equipped to find a killer among the Head Witches, but they deal with rogue beasts all the time."

Beasts. Anger and disgust arose inside me, but Madame Grey stepped in first. "This is a mistake. The thief and the attacker are unlikely to be the same person, and Blair can still help you find the former."

"Based upon what evidence?" said Arabella. "Either the attacker was the same person as the thief, or the attacker was an ally from the other side of the portal the thief took."

"I spoke to every leader of every one of our paranormal communities, and none have seen any signs of any unfamiliar fairies near our homes," said Madame Grey firmly. "Even if the portal *is* within Fairy Falls itself, the people on the other side wouldn't need a man-made portal to access our realm."

Arabella remained unmoved. "I don't know or care how those creatures operate, but I refuse to feel unsafe in my own home. I want my portal back, and I want that attacker behind bars."

I might have asked why she wanted the portal back when she also seemed to think it was spewing assassins who wanted her dead, but that wouldn't do anything to raise me any higher in her estimation. Not that I could sink much lower, but why had she asked me to help in the first place? Had she expected me to readily betray my fellow fairies?

More to the point, the events of the other week had proved why putting the hunters in charge of anything was a monumentally terrible idea. They had one route of action: accuse anyone unfortunate enough to get on their bad side and make arrests without any care for the actual truth. They'd never find the assassin, but that wouldn't stop them from wreaking terror upon Fairy Falls anyway.

"The hunters might have taken the portal themselves," I suggested out of sheer desperation. "What if they wanted to frame the fairies? Or—well, the former Inquisitor *was* a fairy, so they've been fooled before."

Madame Grey shifted on her feet behind me, but I didn't see her expression. On the other hand, Arabella stared at me for a moment before bursting into laughter. "That's the best you can come up with?"

"There were three hunters who used to be allies of Mrs Dailey hanging around the scene where the cabinet was abandoned." My face flushed, but I continued. "I think they're trying to win themselves back into the hunters' good graces by finding the cabinet."

"Nonsense," she said. "Whatever disagreement you might have had with the former Inquisitor, my coven has a long history with the paranormal hunters, and they've rarely steered us wrong."

"Disagreement?" My hackles rose. "He pretended to

be a human for years—decades—and the hunters *did* screw up for you. Why—?"

"Blair has a point about the hunters' untrustworthiness," Madame Grey interjected. Too late, I wondered if she didn't want me to bring up the Inquisitor, but I'd let my anger get the better of me. Arabella seemed to have no understanding of the magnitude of what the Inquisitor had done, unless she simply didn't care.

Arabella shook her head. "I was attacked in my own home, and the hunters are the only people who have a proven track record of bringing magical criminals to justice."

"Or arresting people who *aren't* criminals—which you saw for yourself." Honestly. I might as well have tried to play chess with Thistle the elf.

"I think this is a bad decision," Madame Grey added. "The hunters will not be welcomed either by myself or by Fairy Falls's extensive security team, and the police will never allow them to trespass in our town without cause."

"We'll see," Arabella said. "I think you should both leave—and take that animal with you," she added, indicating Sky, who'd slipped into the room behind me. I hadn't noticed him leave, but he must have gone for a look around the rest of the house, or what was left of it after Arabella had disappeared most of the rooms.

Madame Grey made no further argument. Neither did I. As we left, Arabella tailed us like a cloaked and angry shadow all the way to the front door. Almost as potently present was the sense of utter defeat. The hunters—the *actual* hunters, not Sleepy, Dopey, and Grumpy—were coming back to Fairy Falls.

When we reached the other side of the gates, I crouched beside Sky. "Did you find any clues about who attacked her?"

"Miaow." He hissed at the gates and stalked away.

"Was it a fairy?" I whispered, following at a half crouch to the foot of the hill. "Tap with your front left paw if the answer's yes and your right if the answer's no."

My breath caught when he reached out his left paw and gave a decisive tap on the grass. *It's true. A fairy attacked her.*

It hadn't been someone from Fairy Falls. I *knew* it wasn't, but Arabella didn't see the fairies who lived in my home as any different from the vicious ones who rallied around people like the former Inquisitor and Blythe's mother. Not that she'd acknowledged the former—and speaking of the latter, Blythe would *not* be thrilled at this development. Neither would Nathan, though Madame Grey looked unsurprised at Sky's revelation. "We'll talk about this back at Fairy Falls."

This time I was so flustered when I cast my transportation spell that I nearly did land in the lake. I shuffled out of the shallows to join Madame Grey and recognised the area where the cabinet had been lying the previous day. "Where's the cabinet?"

"I believe our security team picked it up," Madame Grey said. "They'll have taken it to the Enchantment Emporium to see if it can be salvaged or repaired."

"Gus's shop?" I'd forgotten we had a resident expert on magical objects in town. "Might he be able to tell how the thief broke it open?"

"He might," she confirmed. "I'll talk to Steve about strengthening our town's security and preparing for the hunters' arrival."

If I went with her, I had no doubt Steve would pin the blame for the hunters' presence on me—but he wasn't the only one. "I'll warn the fairies, but I don't think they'll take it well."

"It wasn't your fault, Blair," she said. "Arabella already had her theory and was looking for an excuse to send in the hunters."

That didn't make me feel any better. "Does she know what the Inquisitor did?"

"Only as much as the rest of the witch council," she said. "Remember that even most of his own allies didn't know his real identity, Blair, and that he had decades to win the local covens' favour. That won't easily be erased."

"But—does that mean he was close with *her* coven?"

"At one time, yes, and that is precisely why we need to be careful."

On that ominous note, she walked away along the lakeside. A faint meowing drew my gaze to Sky, who sat waiting a short distance away.

"Miaow to you too." I heaved a sigh. "All right. Want to come with me to see Gus?"

"Miaow." He stood up and padded away, heading towards the forest.

"I take that as a no." Perhaps he intended to warn the fairies himself, though I didn't know if they'd be able to understand him.

I wouldn't be able to put off seeing them forever, but Gus might be able to shed some light on what kind of spell had blown open the cabinet. If I confirmed that a witch had been responsible for the theft, it wouldn't let the fairies off the hook for the assassination attempt, but it was better than lying down and letting the hunters walk in.

Gus's Enchantment Emporium seemed aggressively cheerful on a day as dismal as this one, the gold artefacts in the windows glittering under the overcast sky. I pushed the door inwards, and Gus himself appeared in a swirl of glitter worthy of a fairy.

"Blair!" He beamed. "I haven't seen you in ages. How's life?"

"Erm… fine." An honest answer would be too much for the average person to handle, and I didn't need to pile my worries on him. "Did the security team hand you a cabinet earlier today?"

"Yes, they did," he said. "I'm afraid I'll need more time to fix it if you're looking to buy it. It's made of sturdy enchanted wood, but the spell used to dismantle it was a powerful one. I believe the Knotgrass Coven owned it for a century or more—"

"Ah—I'm not looking to buy it," I said hastily. "I'm helping the witches find whoever stole it and dumped it in the lake. Do you know what kind of spell blew it open?"

"Yes, a crude but effective one," he said. "The mechanisms on the door are difficult to open, so someone used the spell equivalent to a battering ram."

A witch? I didn't know if the fairies had a similar spell of their own, but his comment brought another question to mind. The cabinet had been closed when the sceptre had been stolen, and I didn't see Arabella leaving it unlocked when there was a dangerous portal inside.

Did that mean nobody from the other side had taken the sceptre after all? Where was it?

Never mind the sceptre. The clock was ticking, and when the hunters got to Fairy Falls, they wouldn't leave until they had what they wanted.

10

After my visit to the Enchantment Emporium, I met Alissa at the local coffee shop, Charms & Caffeine, where I filled her in on my latest excursion. There weren't many people in the café, since it was the middle of the workday, so we could chat without worrying about being overheard.

"That's absurd," Alissa said when I'd finished explaining Arabella's ultimatum. "How can she have concluded that the best people to solve her problems are the same ones who arrested the wrong person the last time?"

"Apparently I'm just that much of a disappointment." I rolled my eyes. "In all seriousness, I don't think the thief and the attacker were the same person. Or that the attacker came from the other side of the portal either."

"You really think a fairy attacked her, though?"

"Sky thinks so." My chest tightened. "I'm inclined to believe him, though I really wish it were otherwise."

Alissa's brow wrinkled. "Where'd the fairy come from, if not out of the portal?"

"My dad told me the fairies didn't need a man-made portal to move between realms," I said quietly. "It's made for humans to use, not fairies, and finding the portal's thief won't lead her to the person who attacked her."

"But it *will* stop the hunters from coming here." Alissa took a long sip of coffee. "Right?"

"I wouldn't count on it." I drank the rest of my latte. "She's got a major issue with the fairies, and I'm out of ideas on who to question. Though I did wonder if any of the local vampires might remember who gave Arabella's coven the portal in the first place."

Her eyes rounded. "Good point. I can ask Samuel when he's awake, but he's not that old compared to some of the other vampires. You think Vincent might know?"

"He might." The leading vampire claimed to have a bad memory, but one would think that sort of thing would stick in the mind. "The portal was gifted to one of Arabella's predecessors, so they can't have all hated the fairies as much as she does."

Alissa scowled. "What she said to you was uncalled for. She doesn't know you, *or* the fairies."

"No, but she won't accept the possibility that someone else stole that portal." I put my empty mug aside. "Like one of the witches, or even the hunters."

"The hunters?" she echoed. "The ones who showed up by the lake?"

"It's not the least plausible idea," I said. "Arabella doesn't seem to even think the *Inquisitor* did anything wrong. According to Madame Grey, her coven has worked with the hunters for years."

Alissa swore under her breath. "I know Arabella didn't see the Inquisitor get unmasked, but Linda Graham's hunters still let a killer run around her house unchecked. You'd think that would have been a wake-up call."

"I guess she doesn't have any faith in the regular police to deal with this one," I murmured. "She's paranoid enough that she's booted the rest of her coven out of the house too."

"Harsh," she commented. "Do you think *she* framed the fairies?"

I blinked at her. "Why would she dump her own cabinet into a lake in a town she's never lived in?"

"I meant with the attack," she clarified. "The portal's theft might have made her paranoid enough to fake an assassination attempt in order to get attention. I don't know. I'm just throwing out ideas."

I thought back to my last visit. "Sky seemed pretty sure a fairy had been inside the house. It's safe to say I'm disinvited from going back for another look around, so I'll have to work from that assumption. I don't see Sky accusing the fairies without good reason, either."

"True." Alissa rose to her feet to order another drink. While we could theoretically use our menus, from which we simply needed to tap the right order for it to appear on the table, the café often had specials on offer courtesy of Layla, the inventor of the magical instant coffee machine. I went to order another drink, too, picking out a marshberry latte with extra cream.

"Why aren't you at work?" Layla asked over her shoulder as she bustled around making our drinks. She was Lizzie's younger sister and shared the same warm brown skin and curly hair, which she'd braided into a topknot.

"My boss gave me the day off to help avert a crisis." I ought to be doing something more useful than drinking coffee, but I'd already written off the idea of talking to Steve, and that didn't leave me with many other options until the vampires woke up. Except warning the fairies, which I was putting off, but for good reason. How could I break the news that they might no longer be welcome in the very home I'd brought them to in the first place?

"Want me to make you a lucky latte?" Layla placed our drinks on the counter. "Or do you not want to risk the backlash?"

"That… You know, I'm tempted." A lucky latte was good for a short period of luck, but it was invariably followed by a twice-as-long span of catastrophe. Could I count on the latte remaining effective enough to see us through this mess? Debatable.

"It's up to you," she added. "The last person I sold a lucky latte to kept coming back for more even after the backlash. What's that elf's name again, Thistle?"

Alissa reached for her drink. "Why does he want good luck?"

"Something to do with impressing that girlfriend of his. I've no idea," she commented. "I tried to discourage him from ordering lucky lattes, but he kept coming back, so now I'm giving him a placebo instead. He doesn't seem to have noticed yet."

"Yeah, and the rest of the time he's drinking those awful cocktails." I took my drink and returned to the table. "Is that what he was up to by the lake? Sleeping off the aftermath?"

"I doubt drinking cocktails on top of a lucky latte's backlash would have helped." Alissa sat down.

I joined her. "No, but I wish he remembered more about the cabinet being ditched in the lake."

At this point, I was certain the thief was a witch or wizard. The clumsy manner in which the cabinet had been destroyed all but proved a witch spell was responsible, and aside from that time Conor Underwood had lost his temper and unleashed a thunderstorm at me, I'd never seen the fairies use any spells that could be classified as brute force. Arabella, though, wouldn't take Gus's word as proof.

"Yeah." She sipped her drink. "You'd think my grandmother would have her own list of suspects, but now she's had to divert her attention to dealing with preparing for the hunters' arrival in town."

"Exactly." My shoulders slumped. "Arabella has made it harder for us to find the thief by sending the hunters to intervene. They aren't going to find anything, I guarantee. Except a lot of angry fairies, if they walk in and start making accusations."

"Will they even be able to get into their part of the forest?" Alissa asked.

"Good question." Thanks to the fairies' liberal use of glamour, they'd be able to render themselves entirely unseen for the duration of the hunters' visit if they wanted to, but there was no telling to what lengths Arabella would go in order to get answers. "I'm more worried that they'll decide to plant themselves in town until they find the culprit."

"That won't be a popular move."

"Not with most people." I needed to tell Blythe and Rebecca, but the latter was at school, and I didn't know where the former spent her time. I assumed she had a new job, but we had never made small talk with one another, and her recent behaviour had been erratic to say the least. All I knew was that she'd left Fairy Falls for a bit and then come back to live in her mother's old house after Mrs Dailey had been jailed.

Alissa put down her drink. "Speak of the devil. Or elf."

I followed her gaze and watched Thistle walk into the coffee shop. His eyes were half-closed, with the result that he bumped into the doorframe on his way in.

"How dare you!" he said to the door.

"Oh boy," I said in an undertone. "I wonder if he's here for his lucky latte?"

"Poor Layla," she commented. "I think we should help her out."

"Yeah." I rose to my feet to intercept the elf on his tottering way across the room. "Ah—Thistle, how many lucky lattes have you ordered in the past week?"

"None of your concern."

"They don't work when you stack them on top of each other," I told him. "What were you hoping for good luck with in the first place?"

"I told you. It is none of your concern." He sat on the floor. "Where'd the chair go?"

"It's right there." I caught Alissa's gaze, and she shrugged. "You were trying to do something for your girl-friend, right?"

"That's what you told me," Alissa ventured. "In the hospital. You were talking about a special surprise."

"A surprise?" I recalled his odd behaviour the other day. "Is it to do with why you were at the lake?"

He picked himself up off the floor and sat down, once again missing his seat. "It's dodging me, that chair is. Pesky thing."

Honestly. "We're not going to tell Argyle, you know. If you're planning a surprise for her, maybe we can help."

"You would do that for me?" He looked at us beseech-ingly from the floor. "No, I don't trust you humans a bit. You're all scheming and tricksy, you are."

"Not all of us are," I objected. "If you'd rather rely on a lucky latte, then go ahead."

"Now, wait just one second." He got to his feet again, eyeing me blearily. "Mayhap you can help me. I had a gift for my Argyle, but I dropped it in the lake when I was planning the reveal."

"What gift?"

"A present." He sniffed. "A beautiful ring."

Oh boy. "When was this, exactly?"

This was a roundabout way of gathering clues, I'd freely admit, but it would explain why he'd been around the lake at the time when the cabinet had been fished out.

His brow furrowed. "I don't recall, but while I was waiting for her, *they* showed up and startled me."

"Who's 'they'?" I asked. "The people who fished the cabinet out of the lake?"

"Did you talk to them?" Alissa pressed.

"What?" he asked blearily. "It's too early for this questioning. Where's my lucky latte?"

"You already had one," I said. "Several. Thistle, it's important that we know who those people were. Are you talking about the hunters?"

He tried to sit down again and made it into the chair this time. "You're very demanding, aren't you?"

"How about I buy you a lucky latte and you tell me what you heard?" This might backfire on me, but Layla had mentioned switching the lattes for placebos without him noticing, so it was worth seeing if I could bribe him into racking his memory for more clues. "Alissa, you can go and ask Layla to prepare a latte, can't you?"

"Right on it," she said. "If Thistle agrees, that is."

Thistle pouted. "Fine, but you'd better keep your word."

"Of course I will," I said. "What do you remember about the people who startled you?"

"I was near the lake, rehearsing my proposal speech, when I heard humans *laughing* at me." He paused expectantly, as if he wanted me to react.

"That's awful," I said. "They were wrong to do that."

"Obviously," he said. "The noise startled me, so I

dropped the ring. When I was in the water, looking for it, they stood around laughing some more."

"Were they looking for the cabinet?" I asked. "Or was that afterwards?"

"No idea." He yawned. "Where's my drink?"

"It's on its way." I did my level best not to sound too impatient. "Thistle, had they already fished the cabinet out of the water?"

"Oh, they didn't go into the water," he said. "Didn't want to get their shoes wet, I think."

So who got the cabinet out of the water? I supposed one of the merpeople or sirens might have shoved it onto the shore, but how had the hunters known it was there in the first place?

I repeated the question to Thistle, who answered, "They said *she* told them."

My heart lurched. "Who's 'she'? Did they give a name?"

In my experience, there was only one "she" who those three hunters took orders from. *Mrs Dailey.*

"No," he said. "I don't see my lucky latte. Where is it?"

"It's on the way." Alissa indicated the counter. "You've been a great help, Thistle. Did those men you heard mention a portal at all?"

I tensed, but Thistle nodded. "Yes, they were looking for that, too, but they didn't find it."

"They were looking for the portal?" If so, the hunters hadn't been the ones to drop the cabinet... but they'd certainly found out its location quickly.

Thanks to Mrs Dailey. *Who told her, then?* No... I could think of only one explanation for how swiftly she'd obtained the information.

She had spies in Fairy Falls.

"Yes, yes," he said impatiently. "Where's my drink?"

"Here." Layla walked over to his table, carrying a tray containing a mug that overflowed with froth. "I made it just the way you like it."

"Thank *you*." He reached for the mug and didn't look at me again. I knew a losing battle when I saw one, so I returned to my own table.

"What did she give him?" I whispered to Alissa.

"A regular latte spiked with a mild sleeping potion, which ought to keep him out of mischief for a bit."

"Good idea," I muttered. "Looks like the hunters didn't drop the cabinet in the lake, but they were quick off the mark. I think she has spies."

"By 'she,' you mean Blythe's least favourite relative?" She returned to her own drink, her expression preoccupied. "I don't know. Don't forget the lake's huge, and the hunters themselves proved they can get close to the town without technically crossing the border. I doubt the security team would overlook a spy inside Fairy Falls itself."

"No." I picked up my drink. "I'm tempted to try a lucky latte myself, but it'll probably wear off before the hunters get here."

"You don't think you'll need the good-luck boost when you break the bad news to the fairies?"

"Well, yes, but that's not the worst that can happen." The hunters might not get here for hours. "Poor Thistle. It was probably that latte that caused him to drop his ring in the lake."

"Might be worth asking the merpeople if they've seen it." Alissa finished her drink. "Want to go there now?"

"I'd prefer to see Vincent first." I checked the time. Ten thirty. "Do you think he'll be awake?"

"If Madame Grey has told him about the hunters, I think he will be," she replied. "I don't see him neglecting to help his fellow vampires prepare for their arrival."

"True." I drank the rest of my latte. "I'll talk to him first. Want to come with me?"

"Sure, why not. I haven't given Vincent the opportunity to creepily read my thoughts for a bit."

I waved goodbye to Layla, and we got up to leave. On the way, we walked past Thistle, who'd passed out with his chin on top of his not-so-lucky latte.

Outside, I turned to Alissa. "Don't you think it's suspicious that Mrs Dailey's old allies somehow knew there was an abandoned cabinet in that lake?"

"Yes," she replied. "Yes, I think it's suspicious, but Thistle's the one who told us, and I have my doubts the police *or* the hunters would consider him a reliable witness."

"Unless they had faith in my lie-sensing powers," I added. "That would be nice. I suppose I can ask Vincent about that too. He *can* read minds, and he's given evidence in court before."

"True, but those three fools are the least of our problems," she said. "No matter who sent them here, they didn't attack anyone or steal the portal or the sceptre."

"Speaking of the sceptre," I said as we began to walk away from the café, "I forgot to mention that the person who took it might not have come out of the portal, if the cabinet was locked at the time."

"What—someone else in the house took it?" Her eyes widened. "Or Arabella herself?"

"No… She wasn't alone in that room after the arrest, I don't think." Or had she been? She certainly had control over the house's magic. "I'll see what Vincent says about that too."

It was starting to look as if the sceptre's thief wasn't in the fairy realm at all, and if Arabella herself hadn't taken it, did she know the cabinet wasn't the first thing that had been stolen from her house?

Alissa and I reached the top of the hill where the vampires' home lay with the curtains drawn, as was typical during the day. I knocked on the door, and after a short pause, Vincent answered. While he looked tired, his porcelain vampire features were as impeccable as ever, and his suit didn't have so much as a single wrinkle. "Blair. To what do I owe the pleasure of this visit?"

"Ah—have you spoken to Madame Grey today?"

"No," he said. "Oh, you brought a friend too. How nice. Is Samuel treating you well?"

"Er, yes, he is." Alissa looked startled that he'd addressed her directly. "I'm sorry we woke you up, but it's a bit of an emergency."

"So I see." He peered at her face then at mine. "Yes, I do see, despite Blair's steel trap of a mind keeping her thoughts locked within."

"It is?" I hadn't even been trying to keep him out of my head. Most people couldn't shield their thoughts from vampires' mind-reading tendencies easily, but my weird fusion of my parents' magic meant that I could occasionally do so. "You know the hunters are coming to Fairy Falls?"

"Yes, as Madame Grey suspected they would," he replied. "How vexing."

"It's more than just vexing." How much had he read from Alissa's mind? "It's dangerous. Arabella thinks the person who attacked her is *here*, but it's not true."

"That is a dilemma," he agreed, with his usual tendency to understate the issue. "I highly doubt *I* can convince them otherwise, if even the illustrious Madame Grey failed."

My heart sank, though I'd expected that response. "I

thought not, but I wanted to ask a couple of questions about… about Arabella's coven, and the portal into the fairy realm."

"Yes, I was surprised to learn she still had that device in her possession," he said. "Curious."

"She doesn't have it in her possession anymore," I said pointedly. "Did you know which fairy gifted it to her coven? You were alive back then, right?"

"I *have* lived a long time, Blair," he said. "I've met a great number of people, and I cannot say the Knotgrass Coven has ever been of interest to me. Its members are rather bland."

"Vincent." Exasperation spilled into my voice. "I'm sure a fairy giving a portal to a local witch coven is the sort of thing you'd remember."

"Yes…" His expression grew thoughtful. "I remember, but I cannot recall which fairy court was responsible."

"What about Rowe Clearwater?" I threw caution out the window. "Was it *his* court?"

Alissa swore under her breath, while Vincent's gaze sharpened at the name. "It *might* have been."

"Was that a yes or a no?" I took in a breath. "Vincent, you know the—the Inquisitor is on the run and that he might have gone back to the fairy realm. If his old home is on the other side of the portal—that someone in *this* town recently stole—then I'd say it's a cause for concern, wouldn't you?"

"I have long suspected the former Inquisitor has been in the fairy realm, evading attention," he said. "You learned recently that the fairies have no need of man-made portals, didn't you?"

Now he was reading my thoughts. "I did, but someone attacked Arabella. A fairy did, and not a local one."

"Yes… I have to say I don't entirely blame her for

contacting the hunters," he said. "They're crude in their methods, but they're known for finding answers."

"The wrong ones, usually." My temper spiked. "Arabella told me the hunters and her coven have been friends for decades, and you know who's been in charge for most of that time. A fairy masquerading as a human. She doesn't know, or else she doesn't care."

"I imagine it would cause quite the conundrum if she thought on the matter." He retained a calm expression. "If a fairy has marked her as a target, though, there's very little we can do to stop them."

"What?" I stared at him. "If we assume the worst and that the Inquisitor is trying to assassinate powerful witches, isn't that bad news for everyone?"

"There is no shortage of other bad news, Blair," he said. "The former Inquisitor's potential return is a subject I've often discussed with my fellow vampires, and with the rest of the council too."

I'd expected so, but his usual plan for emergencies was to prepare his people to flee the town. Granted, the last time I'd been pleasantly surprised when he'd decided to help out after all, but could I count on him to do the same again?

"There's something else," I said. "The sceptre was stolen too. From the same room as the cabinet."

"So it was," he mused. "Arabella Knotgrass seems to be quite careless with her valuables."

"Yes, and the cabinet was locked at the time," I said. "Does that not ring any alarm bells?"

"An alarm would have been useful, yes." When I groaned, he added, "It's important to have a realistic outlook, Blair. The fairies would have little use for a human artefact like the sceptre, and the immediate issue is the hunters. I *may* be able to assist the witches in preventing them from causing too much trouble in Fairy Falls, if you'll allow me to discuss with my people."

He vanished into the building, while I shook my head again. *Vampires.*

"That was more helpful than I expected," said Alissa. "Where to now? Do you want to warn the fairies?"

"I guess." It was past time I stopped putting off the inevitable and told them the truth about our upcoming visitors.

11

Alissa and I parted ways, though she promised to text me if Samuel gave her any new information that might help us. Since he was a younger vampire than Vincent, though, it was unlikely that he'd have any more insight into whoever had gifted the Knotgrass Coven with a portal to the fairy realm.

Can it be true? Was it really him? Since the Inquisitor had been hiding his real identity for decades, it wasn't entirely implausible that nobody had realised the connection. Even Madame Grey.

I slowed my pace as I reached the forest, still short on ideas as to how to break the bad news without causing a panic. As I slowed, rustling footsteps drew my attention to Aveline ambling along the path just across from me. *She's back here again?*

"Here to see your fairy friends?" she called to me.

"Yes," I said tersely. "Have you spoken to Madame Grey today?"

"Now, why would I do that?" She tutted. "I expect she

already has her hands full dealing with Arabella's paranoia. Let me guess… Arabella sent you packing, didn't she?"

"How did *you* know that?"

Aveline gave a laugh. "There's no need to sound so accusatory, Blair. I heard it from Madame Grey myself."

Had she been eavesdropping on people again? "Then you know the hunters are coming here today too."

"What?" From the shocked note to her barking tone, she *hadn't* known. At least there was one part she hadn't overheard, but maybe I should have left her in ignorance. That way, if the hunters stumbled upon her while searching the forest, they could argue one another into exhaustion rather than bothering the fairies. With a grunt, she stormed down the path, her walking stick thwacking leaves aside. "They need to keep their noses out of our businesses."

"Who's 'our'?" I asked. "You mean the witches?"

"Who else?" she scoffed. "The portal is our property, not the hunters'."

"Hang on, it's not our—it's not the witches' property," I amended. "It's the fairies'. They created it, didn't they?"

"Wrong again," she said. "The portal was created by both a witch *and* a fairy, which might explain why they're so very rare these days."

Since when did she know so much about portals? "If the portal is the witches' property, did one of them steal it from Arabella?"

If there's anything you want to confess to, now would be a great time. This was the third time I'd found her nosing around in the forest for no good reason, and while I managed to refrain from saying so aloud, her eavesdropping tendencies didn't exactly make her look the picture of innocence.

"You're asking the wrong person," was her unhelpful reply.

"Is that what you're looking for in here?" I threw caution to the wind. "Or—the sceptre?"

"Why would you say that?" Aveline said. "Know where it is, do you?"

"No." *Okay, I guessed wrong.* "I don't, but I do know it's not on the other side of the portal, so someone must have taken it before the cabinet was ever stolen."

"You think I want it for myself?" She gave a raucous laugh. "I've earned my retirement from Head Witch duties, don't you think?"

My face flamed. "You're still helping Rebecca, and you know she doesn't want to keep the sceptre—even if she's decided to hang onto it for now."

Another laugh. "Yes, she's very sensible. Much more so than you are."

I frowned at her. "She's more tolerant than I am as well, but that doesn't mean she deserves all this pressure."

"If we all got what we deserved, we wouldn't be in this mess, now would we, Blair?"

She walked off, tramping out of the forest and leaving me more baffled than I'd started out. At least I'd confirmed she wasn't the thief, but I'd been leaning towards that conclusion anyway. She might be a troublemaker and too nosy for her own good, but she didn't fit the profile of the thief *or* the person who'd attacked Arabella.

Shaking my head, I returned to searching out the path to the fairies' part of the forest. In the clearing, my dad answered my knock on his door with such a grave expression on his face that I instantly assumed he must know what news I'd brought.

"Did you hear, then?" I asked.

"Hear what?" He glanced behind him. "I didn't, but your cat has been herding me around for the past hour, so I guessed you had bad news."

"He has?" Sure enough, Sky had planted himself in an armchair in the sitting room. So that's where he'd disappeared to. "You might say I have bad news, yeah. Arabella Knotgrass was attacked by a fairy yesterday. She's sending the hunters in."

Shock blanked out his expression. "No."

Heart twisting, I perched next to my cat and pulled him into my lap. Sky grumbled, but he let me stroke him. "I don't believe for a minute that any of the fairies who live here was involved, but Arabella's sending in the hunters to question everyone. I tried to convince her otherwise, but given the cabinet was found in the lake—she won't bend."

"She thinks the person who attacked her is the same as the thief?"

I inclined my head. "It almost certainly isn't true, but the hunters are not going to find that portal *or* the attacker in the forest. They're wasting their time."

"I have to warn the others." He motioned towards the door. "Unfortunately, Conor is the person the hunters are likely to come across first, since he lives closest to the forest's edge."

"Oh boy." Conor had been in hiding from the hunters for years before I'd tracked him down, and he would not be pleased to learn they'd come back. "You don't deserve to take the heat for my mistake. Let me tell him instead."

"You didn't make any mistakes, Blair," he said. "It sounds as if Arabella and the other witches made their minds up on their own, without any input from anyone else."

"Yeah, but I'm getting nowhere with finding the thief." Not that that would have prevented Arabella from being attacked.

Dad opened the door. "Do you want to wait here while I tell Conor and the others?"

"No… I'll come." I hoped Sky would, too, but he bounded off my lap when I stood up and promptly curled up in my seat.

While Dad and I walked out of the clearing and followed the path to Conor's house, I told him Arabella's account of the attack.

"She's lucky to have escaped," I finished. "But that's not all that I found out today. I spoke to Vincent the vampire…"

"Vincent?" he echoed. "I assume he's less than happy about the hunters coming here too."

"Yes, but he's also old enough to have been here when Arabella's coven was given the portal." I took in a breath, my heart hammering. "He—he can't confirm the identity of the fairy who gave it to her, but he said there's a non-zero chance that the name 'Clearwater' was attached."

Dad stopped walking. "That's impossible."

"Is it?" I tried to see his expression, but his face was turned away from me. "I don't think anyone's actually *used* the portal for decades, but if the former Inquisitor used to be friendly with Arabella's predecessors, it might explain how he was able to hide successfully among humans for so long."

Dad grimaced. "Yes… It would certainly be characteristic of Clearwater to have hidden a portal back to his home inside the property of a local coven while in the guise of a human."

That was exactly what I had been afraid of. "Do you think he was in touch with the fairies he left behind all along?"

"Perhaps." He resumed walking again. "That is a matter we'll have to think on later, after the immediate issue is dealt with."

"Yeah… the hunters." I paused for a moment to collect my thoughts. "And the portal's thief. Unless *that's* him too."

"No… Even if Clearwater *was* the person who gifted the portal to the Knotgrass Coven, it wouldn't make any sense for him to draw attention to himself by stealing something he has no use for."

"I don't think he's careless enough to dump the cabinet in the lake either." The thief had been too clumsy to have possibly been the Inquisitor. "He might have sent someone to act on his behalf, mind, but I've ruled out almost all possible suspects, including those three hunters I found by the lake."

Recognising the street where Conor's cottage lay, I wrenched my thoughts away from the Inquisitor. Nobody had moved in next to Conor, whose cottage was surrounded by trees and isolated from the others. Presumably his need for privacy was a result of his years of living in secret without any of Fairy Falls's other residents knowing he was here, though I'd never asked him directly.

Dad knocked on the red-painted door, while I hovered beside the garden gate and hoped Conor wouldn't hit me with a magical lightning bolt for bringing the hunters back to town. In fact, I was on the verge of backing away when Conor opened the door. Like all the fairies, he had striking pointed features and long silky hair, and his sharp eyes instantly pinpointed me behind my dad. "Blair Wilkes."

"Conor," I said. "Ah, hi."

His gaze slid to my dad. "I assume you brought bad news. You still haven't found that portal?"

"No," Dad replied. "Unfortunately, the witch who owned the portal was attacked by one of our kind yesterday."

Conor's lip curled. "Let me guess, the covens placed the blame upon us."

"Not the covens," Dad corrected. "One witch… who has hired the paranormal hunters to find the culprit."

Conor's entire body went still, tense. "They're coming here?"

"I don't know who attacked her," I blurted, despite my mind shrieking at me to hold my tongue. "I don't think the attacker came from the other side of the portal either, but the cabinet was found in the lake, and——"

"And the witches assumed we were responsible." He cut through my babbling. "Does this Arabella Knotgrass have no knowledge of the hunters' own history with our kind?"

"No," I said. "Well—a little, but Arabella isn't from here, and she doesn't know the details of what happened a few months ago, with—with the Inquisitor."

An expression like thunder shadowed Conor's face. *"Him."*

"Yeah." My throat went dry. "I don't want to cause the others to panic, but if he's involved, then——"

Without waiting for me to finish my sentence, Conor vanished into his house, moving as fast as a vampire. The door thudded closed behind him, and I winced. "That went well."

"I expected him to react in that way," said Dad. "Give him ten minutes, and he'll come back to discuss strategies for keeping the hunters from causing too much damage."

"Can't you keep them out of the forest altogether?"

"That would depend on the strength of our glamour," he replied. "I'll talk to the others."

As we left Conor's cottage behind, I lowered my gaze to the path. "Who else lives out here?"

"Oak," he answered, referencing the eccentric fairy who lived in a toadstool-shaped house elsewhere in this part of the woods. "He won't take the news well."

"He might try to leave."

"He might," Dad agreed, "but the children will talk him out of leaving. He won't want to distress them."

Would the hunters even be able to find his house? Debatable. While they did have sharp eyes that were tuned in to the magical world, most couldn't see through fairy glamour. It would serve them right if they fell into one of his magical traps.

Dad and I walked in silence for a few minutes until I had an abrupt and horrifying thought. "Dad—if it turns out the former Inquisitor *was* friendly with the Knotgrass Coven, does that mean he's familiar with the layout of Arabella's house?"

"Likely… yes."

My pulse began to race. "Her house is covered in a spell that seems designed to confuse people, but the attacker got around it. So did the thief." And so had the person who'd taken the sceptre.

Dad was silent for a long moment before he spoke again. "I wish I knew more. If I hadn't been so isolated from my own people for so long, I might have guessed the connection between the portal and the other activities in the region. It wouldn't surprise me if Arabella Knotgrass's coven played a part in Inquisitor Hare's rise to prominence, like Mrs Dailey's did."

"Me neither," I said sourly. "Speaking of Mrs Dailey, I think she's spying on Fairy Falls. She knew the cabinet was in the lake. Her former hunter allies mentioned that 'she' sent them there too."

"That's concerning." His expression shadowed. "I'm certain that none of the fairies here would ever work with her, but others might be more easily manipulated."

"Like the elves?" Thistle came to mind, but he was far too unreliable to be an effective spy. Besides, his account of the events by the lake hadn't tripped up my lie-sensing powers.

"I doubt it," my dad said, "but I'll send someone to warn the elf king of the hunters' visit."

"Good thinking." They wouldn't take the news well if it came from me, though the same could be said of the fairies.

Unfortunately, when we reached the clearing, we found the other fairies had come out of their houses to watch our return. Ani approached me first.

"Is it true?" she asked. "Are the hunters coming to drive us out?"

"No—no, they aren't." I took in the others' crestfallen expressions, my heart sinking. "They're coming to search for something that was stolen from the Knotgrass Coven, and they'll leave as soon as they're sure it isn't here."

"Looking for what?" asked Ani. "Why would they assume *we* stole it?"

"Because it originally belonged to the fairies." I might have told her and Rosalind about the attack if we'd been alone, but after Conor, I didn't trust myself not to screw up and panic everyone. "Don't worry—the hunters can't see through glamour, so I doubt they'll even be able to get into this part of the forest."

"We can reinforce the glamour around the clearing," Dad added. "As long as none of us leaves, we should be all right. Blair can tell us when the coast is clear and the hunters have gone."

"Of course." Dad was far more equipped to reassure the others than I was, and while I hated that their trust in me had been shaken, I needed to stay on the outside if I wanted to intercept the hunters when they showed up. "I'll talk to Nathan. I bet he and the security team have a plan to send the hunters packing by now."

I'd texted him earlier, but I knew that he'd be busy trying to wrangle Steve and the rest of the security team to put a game plan together. As I left the clearing, my phone buzzed with a well-timed reply from Nathan, asking me to meet him outside of the forest.

I reached the path near the lake, where Nathan greeted me with the strangely reassuring words: "Steve's on the way to the border with a contingent of gargoyles."

"Oh, good." I hugged him. "Are they planning to stop the hunters from getting into the town altogether?"

"That's what I'm hoping." He hugged me back then released me and paced across the lakefront. "That doesn't mean he'll keep them away from the lake or the forest, though."

My hands curled into fists. "It'll serve them right if they get dragged underwater by sirens or speared to death by the elves' pointy sticks."

"I don't disagree," he said. "The shifters are a possible point of concern, but I saw Madame Grey going into the forest to talk to them earlier."

"Chief Donovan definitely won't be thrilled if they intrude on his territory."

"Exactly," Nathan said. "The trouble is that we don't know which direction the hunters intend to approach the town from. If they try to get in through the forest in the north, they'll walk straight into the pack's territory. They might be familiar with the geography, though, in which case they'll approach from the south instead."

"True." I studied the light reflecting on the surface of the lake. "I've had a morning of it. I spoke to that elf again —Thistle—and he confirmed those three hunters were sent by Mrs Dailey. Which means she's spying on the town."

"Are you sure that elf is a reliable witness?"

"No, but I'm inclined to believe him on this one," I said. "You know Mrs Dailey was already trying to recruit allies from behind bars. Sending in spies isn't a stretch."

"True. I've been trying to tell Steve that she's been too quiet lately, but you know what he's like," said Nathan. "He won't accept evidence unless it's knocking on his door."

"Like the hunters." I glanced up as several large winged shapes passed overhead. At least the hunters' arrival here had prompted the gargoyles into action, but what if the hunters weren't the most dangerous threat Fairy Falls faced? "That's the problem. Arabella thinks the hunters are infallible and that the mess with the Inquisitor was just a harmless misunderstanding. I also… I also think her coven has known him for a long time, and in both of his guises."

His eyes widened as the meaning sank in. "As a fairy, you mean? I thought Arabella disliked them."

"Not her—whoever the portal originally belonged to." I spoke quickly. "I talked to Vincent, and he didn't reject my theory that the portal was gifted to Arabella's coven by a certain ex-Inquisitor. Dad thinks it's possible too."

Nathan swore. "Possible? Not definite?"

"You know how hard it is to get a straight answer out of a vampire," I said. "It was decades ago, and he's not local to her coven, but my dad said it would have been a convenient way for the Inquisitor to keep in contact with the fairies in his own realm while he was masquerading as a human. He wouldn't have needed an excuse to pay frequent visits to a coven with whom the hunters were closely allied."

Comprehension dawned on him. "If that's true, do you think he's the one who stole the portal?"

"No… I don't know." I faltered. "This is all speculation, and Madame Grey won't take it as proof, but we already know that the fairies don't need portals to travel between realms. Also, the person who attacked Arabella might have been after the portal as well, without knowing it had been taken."

"Yes… not many people knew she owned it until recently, and it's no wonder, if the original recipient is long dead or retired," Nathan said.

"The fairies are immortal, though, so the person who gifted the portal to her is probably alive and kicking," I reminded him. "We're not dealing with people with normal life spans here."

Nathan swore under his breath again. "If it *is* him… The hunters are supposed to be on alert for his return. The order is that he's to be taken immediately to the LPFP if anyone sets eyes on him again."

"Have the hunters considered what he's capable of, though?" I asked quietly. "He's a fairy. He can use glamour to hide himself, and he also has in-depth knowledge of how the hunters work."

"He does," he agreed, "which means the hunters are far more vulnerable than they're aware."

"And to think they're wasting their time coming here instead." I glanced down at our reflections on the surface of the lake. From the outside, we looked like an ordinary human couple—not an ex-hunter and a half fairy. Appearances could be deceptive. If there was one lesson the magical world had drilled into me, it was that. "This feels… final. Like something's about to happen that we can't go back from."

"Don't say that, Blair." His hand slid into mine. "We'll get through this. We always do."

I rested my head on his shoulder for a moment. "I know, but… This is all happening so fast, and there are too many moving pieces to keep our eyes on. Even Madame Grey can't make the Inquisitor or Mrs Dailey her main priority, and who can blame her? If the hunters move in and take over Fairy Falls, she loses everything."

"Exactly," he said. "The security team is taking this seriously, though. My sister is furious."

"I bet," I said. "I take it the hunters won't react well if I tell *them* the Inquisitor might be manipulating everyone from the fairy realm?"

"Definitely not," he replied. "Most of them won't discuss the former leader at all. They're too ashamed."

"At being taken in," I said. "But they're being taken in again, right this instant, and if nobody warns them…"

Nobody else could. I'd have to warn them myself, even if they didn't believe me.

Nathan released my hand. "Not alone, Blair. I have to go and find the rest of my team, but you won't do anything reckless, will you?"

"I could say the same to you." Our brief moment of calm was over. It was time to fight.

While he went to convene with his fellow security team members, I made for the coven's headquarters. The clamour of voices reached my ears as soon as I opened the door, and I found the lobby packed with witches. It looked like the entire council was gathered in front of their usual meeting room, including Rita and Madame Grey.

Upon spotting me, the latter made her way over to the door. "There you are, Blair. My granddaughter told me you were warning the fairies."

"I did—but where's Rebecca?" I asked.

"At school," she replied. "I'd prefer for her not to know about this until after we've sent the hunters packing."

Her certainty surprised me. "That's the plan? You don't think they'll be able to get in?"

"Not if I can help it," she said. "If they are truly as law-abiding as they claim, they'll have to talk directly to the covens or the police before they'll be allowed to hassle any of our civilians. Including the fairies."

"I don't have that much faith in them to follow the rules." Given the assembled witches in the lobby, all of whom carried their wands, the rest of the coven didn't seem to, either. "Nathan said you warned the werewolves in case they come through the forest too."

"We did," she confirmed. "The shifters are watching the northern border, but the hunters are more likely to approach from the southern border, near the lake."

"Nathan said the same." I drew in a breath. "Are they already on the way?"

She inclined her head, and the last of my hopes evaporated. "They are."

"But—I have something else to tell you too." Worries swarmed in my chest like a hive of bees. "I don't want to distract from this, but those three hunters we saw the other day—"

"Later, Blair." She turned her attention towards the front door. "Do you want to stay here, or would you rather head to the border with the rest of the security team?"

"I—" I hesitated, torn. "I'll go to the border. I doubt Steve would be happy for me to be there, but maybe I can find a reasonable hunter who'll be willing to talk."

The odds weren't great, but I didn't belong here with the witches or even in hiding with the fairies.

I was a fairy and a witch both, and I was going to defend my home.

12

I caught up to Nathan and the rest of the security team near the southern border. Upon seeing me, surprise flickered across his face. "Did Madame Grey send you?"

"No, she gave me the choice as to how to make myself the most useful." I sucked in a breath. "I'm going to talk to the hunters myself."

He opened his mouth as if to argue and then nodded. "If you're sure."

Erin caught my eye from in front of him, looking unusually grim. "I'm more in favour of you turning them into toadstools than talking to them."

"I don't know that spell, but the fairies might do that if they go into the forest."

"I hope not," Nathan said. "If they do, the hunters will have an excuse to retaliate."

"Won't they do that anyway?" Erin strode ahead of us, her hands in her pockets. "Don't worry, I'll behave. I'm just saying that I wouldn't object if Blair *accidentally* hit them with one of her glitter spells."

"There's always the chance it might actually happen by accident." I didn't quite dare get out my wand yet, and my nerves spiked as we followed the curving path of the lake to the south, where several winged forms stood on the town's boundary.

The gargoyles waited for us in their shifted forms, resembling grey-skinned giants with tails and wings. We gathered nearby, not speaking, and my heart gave a jolt when a group of humans descended the hillside south of the lake. At least ten of them, dressed as if they were about to scale a mountain to slay Bigfoot and armed to the teeth.

As they approached, everyone held their breath. Well, almost everyone.

"You don't have permission to set foot on the other side of the border," Steve said, his booming gargoyle voice reverberating in the air.

The hunters gave no reaction. As they neared, my gaze fell on the woman leading the pack. Linda Graham. *Arabella gave her a second chance?*

"We're here on behalf of the Knotgrass Coven," she called to Steve. "I think you'll find that coven law allows us to enter your town if we believe you're harbouring a fugitive who the paranormal hunters have been ordered to find."

Steve bared his teeth at her. "Prove it."

Linda didn't so much as flinch, but I was very glad not to be on the other end of the gargoyles' glare. While Steve mostly came across as a lazy buffoon, he had no more desire to let the hunters trample all over the town than the rest of us did. *Go on. Drive them off.*

Linda halted in front of the group of gargoyles. "We have undeniable proof that the Knotgrass Coven's head-quarters was infiltrated by a fairy—twice, if you count the theft of a valuable artefact—and the cabinet you removed from the lake proves that they're hiding close to our location."

"You want to search the lake?" Steve jerked his head towards the expanse of water. "If so, you're only allowed to search the part that isn't on our side of the border."

"Bet the merpeople would love that," Erin said in an undertone. "I almost want them to try it."

"Forget the lake," said Linda, a bite of impatience to her voice. "The home of the fairies is our goal, which I'm to understand is in the forest."

"Wrong," said Steve. "The fairies don't live in Fairy Falls."

What? I hadn't expected Steve would have the fairies' back against the hunters, but I'd been so sure he'd had a plan to keep them out. Entering the forest would still involve crossing the border.

"No?" she said. "In that case, you should have no problem with us questioning them."

"You're not to set foot over the border." Steve dug his heels into the ground. "Not on the ground, water, or air."

Oh. They can't get to the fairies without crossing the border. That was a surprisingly observant strategy on Steve's part, though it might not have been his idea. I bit back a laugh at the incredulous expression on Linda's face, though my relief was short-lived.

Linda drew in a breath, her gaze flinty. "Then I demand that all the fairies in this town present themselves here at once."

"You haven't the authority to give *me* orders," Steve growled in retaliation.

"He didn't come up with this on his own, did he?" I whispered to Nathan, who shook his head.

"No," he murmured. "Madame Grey gave him direction."

"Good." Steve wasn't smart enough to talk circles around the hunters, but Madame Grey had anticipated this turn of events. That didn't mean we'd won yet, though.

"This is unacceptable," said Linda. "We have ample evidence that the person who stole the portal from Arabella's property lives behind the borders of Fairy Falls."

"Care to give me a name?"

"Blair Wilkes," she said.

My face flamed as all eyes turned towards me, but I stood my ground. "What? You're accusing *me*?"

"You're still here, then?" she asked, ignoring my question.

"Where else would I be?" I concentrated on Nathan's steady presence at my side rather than the restless whispering amid the gargoyles. "Steve's right—and trust me, this is the first time I've ever been able to say that with a straight face."

Steve scowled, but I ignored him and pushed on.

"You can't come in here and start hassling the civilians without any proof," I told Linda. "The fairies rarely leave their home, and none of them has any reason whatsoever to attack a coven leader they've never met before. Most of them don't even know Arabella's name."

"I find that hard to believe, given how long-lived the fairies are," Linda said. "Furthermore, their ability to trick the senses and use glamour to hide themselves indicates that they cannot be trusted."

"Just because you can't see what's right in front of your face, it doesn't mean the same applies to us," Erin called out. "We have people on our security team who can see through glamour. We'd know if one of the local fairies was going around committing murder."

Linda scowled in her direction. "If so, you're all complicit."

"Now you're accusing the whole town?" Erin raised a brow at her. "If one of the fairies was behind this, I can guarantee certain people would be lining up to tell tales on them."

Nathan gave his sister a look, warning her to simmer down, but I had to admit the flush on Linda's face was highly satisfying to witness.

My brief sense of triumph faded when Linda turned her attention towards me. "You're half fairy, Blair, so we can start with you."

"Arabella *hired* me to help find the thief." I should have known she'd try another angle to weasel her way in. "I was at her house yesterday. She wouldn't have let me in if she thought I'd attacked her the previous day."

"You and Arabella had a history that indicates you have good reason to prevent her from getting her property back," Linda said. "She might not have suspected you of the theft herself, but you wanted to use that portal, didn't you?"

"No. I didn't." Did Arabella? Surely not, but there was no telling what was going through her head at the moment, nor what she'd told Linda. "I was at work when the theft took place, not anywhere near Arabella's house. My boss and co-workers can back me up."

"You're friends with the local fairies, are you not?" Linda said. "You could easily have sent one of them to steal for you."

"I wouldn't have done that to them." Anger flared, though I remained conscious of the other gargoyles and the security team within hearing distance. "Remember a few weeks ago when I found a killer in Arabella's own house? Why would she have hired me to help find the culprit if she thought I was the one who stole the portal in the first place?"

"Exactly," said Erin. "Accusing Blair of all people makes you look ridiculous."

"I beg to differ." Linda turned to Steve. "If I believe Blair is a viable suspect, I have permission to search her property, do I not?"

"Search my—I haven't even been home all week." *Oh. Now I get it. She just wants an excuse to find a loophole in the rules in order to come into Fairy Falls.*

Steve bared his teeth. "Yes, if that were the case, you would be able to search Blair's property for the portal."

"It isn't there." Unless Aveline had stashed it in my room, which wasn't the least likely outcome of this increasingly surreal day. "I'm also loaning my room to the former Head Witch, Aveline Hollyhock, so I haven't been at home in over a week."

"Aveline Hollyhock is here?" Linda's smug expression dissipated at the name.

"Yes, Blair has a cranky former Head Witch crashing in her room," Erin put in. "Feel free to go there anyway if you want her to hex you."

Clearly, nobody had informed Linda of our unwanted guest. "Then where is Blair living now?"

"At my house," Nathan answered.

"I don't think you're being truthful." Linda turned to me. "Why exactly is the Head Witch staying in your home?"

"Aveline Hollyhock is currently training Rebecca as Head Witch, and no other accommodation was acceptable to her. You're welcome to go there and ask her yourself."

I almost hoped she would, as if she got into a fight with Aveline, she was more likely to forget about the fairies altogether... But that would still involve her setting foot in Fairy Falls.

Linda considered this and then asked Steve, "Would that be acceptable?"

"I suppose it would be," he growled.

No. Once the hunters had a reason to get into the town, they wouldn't leave. Steve knew that as well as I did. Why would he cave in? Did he think so little of me that he was willing to risk the other townspeople's safety to see me humiliated?

Linda Graham beckoned to two of the other hunters. "Come with me, and we'll search Blair's property. The rest of you wait by the border until we hear from the head office."

What does that mean? Were they trying to obtain extra permissions to wrangle their way into the fairies' home? I caught Nathan's eye and saw a glint of anger, but he shook his head when Erin made to waylay the hunters. He knew they'd won this round.

As Linda and her two allies walked into Fairy Falls, I followed them, determined not to let them out of my sight. Nathan walked at my side, though his sister and Buck stayed at the border. To watch the other hunters, I assumed.

At the foot of the hill, Linda glanced over her shoulder at me. "Lead us to your house, Blair. I wouldn't recommend misleading us."

"I wouldn't dream of it."

Crossing my fingers that Aveline was taking a nap or out walking in the woods, I intentionally took a route through the main high street and past the witches' headquarters on my way home. As I'd hoped, Madame Grey and the other witches were ready and waiting.

"What is the meaning of this?" Madame Grey marched out to meet Linda and the hunters. "You shouldn't be in Fairy Falls."

"I am here to search the property of a suspected thief," said Linda. "Blair Wilkes."

Madame Grey's eyes narrowed as she processed the trickery the hunters had pulled. "Then be quick about it, and if you set foot anywhere else in this town, I'll personally escort you to the border."

Linda appeared unaffected by the threat, motioning to me to lead the way forwards again. "Go on."

Resigned, I led the way to the house and opened the front door. A bemused Alissa peered out of our flat, eyes rounding at the sight of our visitors. I peered behind her, but I didn't see Aveline.

"Blair," Alissa whispered to me as the hunters marched past and into the living room. "What's going on?"

"The hunters think I stole the portal," I told her in an undertone. "They wanted an excuse to get into Fairy Falls. Where's Aveline?"

"I don't know."

"Back in the forest, I bet." I winced when Aveline's two companions heaved the sofa onto its side to search underneath, causing Roald to yowl and flee the room. At least Sky was still at my dad's cottage, as far as I knew. "I hope this puts Aveline off coming back."

Linda Graham planted herself in front of the window while her two companions turned the flat inside out. I knew this whole act was intended to intimidate us. They didn't actually believe the portal was here, and it was unsurprising when Linda led the others out of the house without so much as an apology.

"I'll fix the damage, Blair," Alissa whispered as I made to pull out my wand. "You make sure they leave town."

"There's a higher chance of Aveline starting a charity for orphans." I followed the hunters' path out of the house, where Nathan waited for me.

Linda was already departing at speed, but I hurried to catch up to her. "Where are you going?"

"To question our next suspects," she replied. "Am I right in thinking most of the fairies live in the forest?"

I knew it. "You won't find them in there. You *might* find a bunch of angry elves, though—or werewolves."

"Blair, I don't think you're being honest with me." She gave me a piercing look. "If you won't lead me to them, I'll make my own way."

While she presumably hadn't been here before, the forest wasn't exactly hard to miss. Linda led her two allies away from the high street, ignoring Nathan and me altogether.

"This is going to end well," I muttered to him. "They won't find anything in the forest except angry elves and shifters."

"Exactly," he said. "If they object, things might get ugly."

"Same if Conor hits them with a thunderstorm." While he'd mellowed in the past few months, there was no telling what he might do if the hunters found his house.

As we walked, I kept both eyes open for the fairies' path to the woods, but it wasn't in its usual place. Since the hunters weren't looking at me, I tilted my head and attempted to pick out the glamour hiding it from sight, but no signs of the path appeared. *Dad and the others must have worked their magic.*

Not that the hunters would be easily deterred. After they'd walked straight through the woods to the lake and back again, Linda beckoned to me. "Take us to the fairies, Blair Wilkes. You know where they are."

I shook my head. "You won't believe me, but I don't."

Linda tutted. "Now, I did tell you not to lie to me, didn't I?"

"You are not welcome," said a sudden voice that did *not* belong to a fairy.

One of the hunters jumped, while even Linda looked startled to see the three-foot-tall figure walk out of the nearby undergrowth. Bramble. Several other elves gathered amid the trees, armed with pointed sticks. *Uh-oh.*

"That's not for you to decide." Linda looked down at Bramble. "We're looking for the home of the fairies."

"You dare to presume to give us orders?" Bramble said, to a chorus of angry mutters from his fellow elves. "That is a grievous insult. We take instruction only from our king."

Linda's fellow hunters exchanged uneasy glances, but she pushed on. "Then take me to your king. He'll likely have heard of us before."

"We do not permit humans to enter our home without permission," Bramble said. "We have lived here for many centuries, long before the paranormal hunters ever existed."

Yet more elves popped up on either side of the path. Half the elf king's contingent seemed to have volunteered to drive the hunters out of town. Linda reached for a weapon and then hesitated when the elves raised their pointed sticks in retaliation.

"You will not find what you seek in here," Bramble growled. "Tread carefully."

His words might not sound threatening coming from a three-foot-tall elf, but Linda's two companions backed further away with each word he spoke.

Linda lifted her chin. "I *will* find the fairies, regardless of whether you help me or not."

"You have no authority over us," another elf said. "Nor the shifters, and if you trespass on either of our territories, we will ensure you pay."

Was I hearing right? Had the elves and the werewolves

come to an agreement? Even Linda's expression showed uncertainty, especially when she noticed her fellow hunters had backed away down the path and left her alone to face the elves.

"You aren't going to find the fairies in here," I told her. "They live somewhere outside of the town altogether—out of this world, in fact—and as long as they don't want to be found, even I can't take you to them."

"She speaks true," said Bramble, and the elves chorused their agreement.

Linda glared at me, but the fire in her eyes had dimmed. "We will find what we seek eventually, Blair Wilkes. That I promise you."

She turned and swept away, following her fleeing companions. The elves flanked the hunters from both sides of the path, and I didn't quite dare breathe out until they were out of the forest's boundaries.

I should have felt relief at their departure, but the absence of the fairies' path lingered like an itch I couldn't scratch. As the danger faded, the truth sank in. I'd told my dad I'd come and inform him and the fairies when the coast was clear, but how was I supposed to do that if I couldn't see through the glamour hiding the clearing?

As the elves returned to the woods, I waylaid Bramble. "Erm, thank you for helping us."

"We did not do this as a favour to you."

I figured. "Still, I'm grateful. I don't suppose you know how to find the fairies again?"

"No. I did not lie, as you should know well."

"Of course you didn't, but I need to tell them the coast is clear…" Was it, though? The hunters had left the woods, but there was no telling whether they'd change their minds and come marching back in.

Bramble apparently didn't think so, because he

vanished into the bushes among the other elves. Heart pounding, I tracked down Nathan at the forest's entrance. "Can you make sure the hunters leave? I want to find the fairies."

"You can wait until later, can't you?" he asked. "Until they've left?"

"Yeah, but I don't like not being able to see through the glamour." A flash of glitter caught my gaze, and I saw the pixie hovering above a bush. Nathan watched in puzzlement while I ran over. "Hey—can you take me to the others? Can you find them?"

The pixie shook his head.

"What do you mean, no?"

"You still know little of your own kind, Blair Wilkes," Bramble growled, and I jumped, not having realised he was still there.

"What's that supposed to mean?" I pivoted towards the elf. "You already told me you can't find them either."

"Yes, because they shut their doors against outsiders," he said. "That includes you, Blair."

This time he did vanish, while my heart plunged into my shoes.

I couldn't get to my dad. We were literally a world apart.

13

I stayed in the forest for a while, searching for the fairies, but without any luck. As I was staring at the path with stinging eyes, Nathan approached me from behind and wrapped me in a hug. "Come on, Blair. Let's go. They'll be back before you know it."

"Yeah." I blinked hard. "I know they're safer… wherever they are, but I didn't expect them to completely vanish outright. And will it ever be safe for them to come back?"

"It will," he promised. "We'll see what we can do to make it safe. Promise."

I checked the time, realising it wouldn't be long before Rebecca was out of school. Then she'd find out the hunters had been here, if she didn't already know. She didn't deserve to hear it from Aveline, so I reluctantly followed Nathan out of the forest. To my surprise, Erin and Buck waited for us. They must have left the border when the hunters had departed.

"They're really gone?" Erin asked. "The fairies?"

"Not forever." My firm tone was more to convince myself than the others. "I forgot that I wouldn't be able to tell them the coast was clear if I couldn't actually get to them."

"I can look," offered Buck.

I doubted he'd be able to find the path if I couldn't see it with my sharper eyes, but I decided not to say so aloud. "I doubt they'll come back until they're sure the hunters are gone."

For all we knew, Linda would come straight back tomorrow and try again. She hadn't found the stolen portal *or* identified Arabella's attacker, and unless someone came up with an alternative, we were her only suspects.

We walked away from the forest, where I spotted Steve the gargoyle on the street ahead, back in his human form but no less intimidating without his wings. Upon seeing me, he bared his teeth. "Don't think I'm going to forget this, Blair Wilkes."

"I didn't bring the hunters here," I protested. "I tried my best to keep them away."

"Then you did a terrible job."

"Don't be ridiculous, Steve," Nathan said. "If you want to talk to the person who sent the hunters here, ask Madame Grey to put you in contact with Arabella Knotgrass."

Hmm. That might be a good idea… or a terrible one.

"Really," Steve said in flat tones. "Would the hunters have come here to interrogate the fairies if *she* hadn't brought them here to begin with?"

Okay, that was unfair. "The local fairies aren't to blame for this. You know that as well as I do."

"I notice they aren't stepping up to defend themselves," he growled. "On that note, it seems odd for them to call themselves citizens of Fairy Falls when they don't live within our borders, doesn't it? Especially when their presence here puts other citizens at risk. Don't you agree, Blair?"

My heart gave a sickening dive. "You can't revoke their right to live in Fairy Falls."

"No, you certainly can't," Nathan put in. "You're out of line, Steve."

The gargoyle glowered at him. "Ask yourself what you would do if another citizen of the town attacked someone."

"You know every fairy in existence doesn't live in Fairy Falls, don't you?" I asked. "They didn't attack anyone."

"If you want to prove their innocence, Blair Wilkes, I suggest you find the person who *did* attack Arabella Knotgrass. It can't be that steep a task, can it?"

"Isn't it *your* job to catch criminals?" With the others at my back, my confidence was bolstered, and Steve's bluster was nothing I couldn't handle. "I spoke to Gus at the Enchantment Emporium, and he said the portal's cabinet was destroyed by a spell cast by a witch, not a fairy. The thief might be here, but the attacker isn't."

Steve remained unmoved. "I don't want to hear any more from you, Blair Wilkes. I want you three to come with me and put together a team to send to the border in order to make sure no more intruders try to sneak in."

Ignoring me, he ushered the others towards the police station. Nathan gave me a sympathetic look, and I managed a smile in response before Steve closed the doors between us.

What now? The hunters might have gone, but until I found the real thief, we were only postponing their next visit. Without access to the fairies, I couldn't ask them for ideas either.

I went to the witches' headquarters in search of Madame Grey, but before I reached the doors, I found

Blythe trying to drag Rebecca down the street by her arm, while her sister put up an impressive resistance.

"Stop that!" Rebecca was saying. "I'm not leaving."

"Leaving?" I echoed, catching up to her sister. "What are you doing?"

"I could ask you the same question," said Blythe. "Why didn't you tell either of us that the hunters were coming to town?"

"They aren't here now," I said. "What do you mean, why didn't *I* tell you? Couldn't you have asked Madame Grey?"

"You're the one who brought them here." She released her sister's arm and faced me defiantly. "What if they'd arrested Rebecca again?"

"They came because they thought *I* stole the portal," I corrected. "I'd never have let them in if I thought Rebecca was in any danger. Madame Grey thought she'd be safer if she stayed at school."

"They thought you were the thief?" Rebecca said blankly. "Didn't Arabella *hire* you?"

"Yes, but the hunters blamed all the fairies, including me," I said. "They didn't genuinely think I was the thief, but it was a convenient excuse for them to get into the town. That Linda Graham is sneaky, I'll say that much."

"*She* was here?" Blythe's face went brick red. "I can't believe you let *her* in after what she did to my sister."

"I can speak for myself, you know," said Rebecca. "She didn't threaten to arrest the other fairies, did she?"

"No—the fairies hid their home using glamour," I explained. "They're fine, but I have to find the actual thief before the hunters come back or Steve revokes the fairies' citizenship—whichever comes first."

"He can't do that." Rebecca backed away from her

sister's outstretched hands. "You can't take me away from here either."

"Take you away?" I swivelled back to Blythe. "You weren't going home?"

"Not that it's any of your business," said Blythe, "but I think we'd be safer somewhere else."

My heart seized. "You want to leave town?"

"*I* don't," Rebecca said. "Give it a rest, Blythe. I want to stay."

"What's the point in dragging her away from town now?" I asked her sister. "Rebecca still has the sceptre, and she's much safer if she stays here."

"Not from them." Blythe lifted her chin. "You don't get to judge me for wanting to get somewhere that isn't swarming with hunters and fairies."

"Swarming?" I knew she was reacting out of anger, but her comment hit a raw nerve. "That sounds like your mother talking."

I'd meant for my words to sting as much as hers had, but Rebecca was the one whose eyes brimmed with tears. Guilt hit me at once, but Blythe pulled out her wand. "How dare you!"

"I just meant you *sounded* like her." I didn't grab my own wand, though I was prepared to snap my fingers and fly out of reach if she decided to curse me.

Rebecca planted herself in front of her sister's wand hand. "Stop it."

Ignoring her sister, Blythe said, "My mother worked *with* the fairies who committed crimes. All I want to do is get Rebecca away from them. I want an apology."

"Then apologise to me." Rebecca stood in her sister's path. "I don't like being argued over like an inanimate object, and the sceptre would draw attention even if I went to the other side of the planet. You don't think there aren't people waiting to assassinate me as soon as I go outside of Madame Grey's sight?"

"Exactly." Aveline Hollyhock came ambling around the corner. "She has more sense than you do. Both of you."

"Where have you been all this time?" I hadn't seen her in the forest, so who even knew where she'd wandered off to. "It'd be nice if you actually made an effort to help us out rather than eavesdropping on people and then disappearing whenever things might get dangerous."

"You seemed to do a fine job of sending the hunters packing on your own, without any need for my input," she said. "As for your dilemma, Rebecca, you *can* leave town if you give up the sceptre."

"Now?" Rebecca turned away from her sister, who sheepishly lowered her wand. "I thought we weren't ready. You said we couldn't afford to lose another Head Witch."

"Did you now?" I asked Aveline. "Are you *sure* you don't want to claim it for yourself?"

"If there's no other option, I will take on the burden myself."

Burden? Yeah, right. She might have told the truth when she'd said she had a more relaxed life without the sceptre, but she still coveted it as much as she always had. "What if the sceptre doesn't pick you?"

"That won't be a concern."

"I thought the whole point of Rebecca giving up the sceptre was to give her a choice," I said. "It sounds more like you're manipulating Rebecca into handing the sceptre directly to you."

The worst part was that I could see her point. I'd be glad to foist the sceptre off on Aveline if it meant giving Rebecca a shot at a normal childhood, but the sceptre itself had chosen her, and Aveline wasn't as strong as she'd once been. Besides, it *was* ultimately Rebecca's choice.

"She doesn't want it, does she?" Aveline turned to Rebecca. "Do you?"

"No," she said, "but I don't want to leave Fairy Falls. If… If our mother really does come back, I'd rather have the sceptre than be defenceless."

My attention snapped over to Blythe. "Yes, about that. Did you know your mother was spying on Fairy Falls?"

"This is news to you?" Blythe scoffed. "You already knew she's been recruiting for a while."

Dread gripped me. "That's why you're running. Not from the hunters, but from *her*."

"The hunters are in my mother's pocket whether they realise it or not," she retaliated. "I'm not running for my own sake. I'm protecting my sister."

"You won't be any safer from the hunters no matter where you run to," I said. "Are you implying that you think your mother is an immediate threat? If there's anything you haven't shared with the rest of us, at least tell Madame Grey. Didn't the incident a few weeks ago teach you that keeping things to yourself isn't a good idea?"

"No," she snapped. "No, it taught me the potential consequences of secrets getting out."

"What, you mean Arabella's portal being stolen?" I gave her a pointed look. "Did she have someone take it? If you know where it is—"

"That's not what I meant," she interjected. "Arabella had no idea of its true value, but others did. Imagine what might happen if my mother's allies gained a way to bring an army of fairies anywhere they wanted to."

"They wouldn't need a portal for that." I regretted my words when the colour drained from Rebecca's face. "I mean, they don't need a portal to travel between realms. I don't think they have an army."

Blythe made a startled noise. "What?"

"What do you mean, what?"

"Fairies don't need to use a portal to travel from one realm to another?" she asked. "Since when?"

"You didn't know that? I thought your mother—"

"That's enough," she growled under her breath. "She didn't teach me about the fairies, not in any way that matters. You'd better not be lying."

"Why would I?" Had she assumed her mother wanted to summon up an army of fairies to help her stage a jail-break or something? "My dad told me himself that the fairies can travel between one realm and the others without any need for a man-made portal. That's how they hid their part of the forest, and it's also why leaving town won't help you escape them."

Blythe drew in a breath then addressed Rebecca. "If you don't want to leave town, you can come home with me."

"No!" she said. "I don't want to go to our mother's house."

Blythe's jaw tensed, her eyes glittering with fury. "It's safer there. I know spells that can keep even the fairies from getting into the house."

"It'd be nice if you shared them with the rest of us," I said as Aveline gave an inexplicable cackle. "What? Do you find us amusing?"

"Yes, as a matter of fact, I do," she said. "Have you forgotten the hunters are still at the border?"

"No, I haven't." I'd also had about enough of her atti-tude. "If you don't have anything constructive to add, then leave us alone."

"Impertinence." Her lip curled. "If you change your mind about the sceptre, you know where to find me."

She hobbled off, while Blythe moved protectively in front of her sister. "You can go away, too, Blair."

"I'm not letting you off the hook," I said. "You keep trying to avoid me, but you know what your mother's up to, don't you? Three of her hunter allies were near the lake the other day—Sleepy, Grumpy, and Dopey—and they all but admitted they had spies in Fairy Falls."

"Why didn't you tell me that?" Her spine went rigid. "That means they're back in the region."

"We already worked that out for ourselves," I said. "You ran off when I tried to tell you, in case you've forgotten. *Do* you think your mother is going to make a move?"

"Does it matter?"

"I take that as a yes." I folded my arms across my chest. "You aren't trying to fight. You're running away. Why?"

She shot me a glare that pinned me to the spot. "Because the Inquisitor is back, as you figured out yourself. When I say it's a matter of time before he comes here, I'm not being defeatist, I'm being realistic. If he doesn't have to use the portal to get here, nothing can keep him out."

The world tilted under my feet, her words echoing like a premonition. *He's back. I was right.*

"If you knew," I croaked. "If you'd told me, we could have made a plan—"

"There's no 'we.'" Once more, she turned her gaze towards her sister. "Rebecca, I have to take care of something, but I'll come back. Please at least consider coming back to the house. I'll be there if you change your mind."

She speed walked away, while her sister watched in confusion that matched mine.

"What was that about?" I asked.

Rebecca shook her head, while I wondered if her sister intended to flee after all. It was better than her dragging Rebecca along with her, though not much. Blythe was justified in being upset and scared, but I wished she didn't insist on acting alone.

I guess she still doesn't trust us, even after all this time.

I had to wonder, though, why she'd reacted the way she had to the news that the portal had no effect on the fairies' ability to cross between realms. Had she assumed the Inquisitor had been held back by the one known portal in the region being in Arabella's hands until recently? If Blythe had some way of protecting herself and her home from the fairies, why was she so fearful of an imminent attack?

Unless… Unless she *did* know where the portal was.

14

As I made to follow Blythe, Vincent the vampire appeared, forcing me to an abrupt halt to avoid walking straight into him. "Whoa."

"I see you successfully drove off the hunters, Blair," said Vincent.

"That won't last, you know it won't." I tried to step around him, but the vampire glided into my path once more. "I don't suppose *you* know how I can get the fairies to come back… Wait, can you contact Sky?"

My heart lifted and then sank when the vampire shook his head. "Don't worry yourself, Blair. I doubt that cat of yours will allow himself to be stuck anywhere he doesn't want to be."

Easier said than done. "Well, I hope they come back soon. Steve's threatening to remove the fairies' citizenship of the town altogether if they don't."

"Yes, that is a dilemma," he said. "I should congratulate you on figuring out who took the portal, however."

"I—wait, how did you know? I thought you couldn't read my mind."

"Your face is quite transparent." He flashed me a brief smile and vanished, leaving a blurred impression on my eyelids. *Vampires.*

Shaking off the bewilderment of his unexpected interruption, I resumed following Blythe. She was closer than I'd expected—she must have lingered to eavesdrop on Vincent and me—but when she saw me watching her, she took off at a fast stride.

I quickened my pace and followed Blythe uphill to her mother's house. From what I could see of the garden behind the gate, it looked somewhat unkempt compared to when her mother had lived there.

"Blythe." I caught up to her as she pushed the gates open and walked into the overgrown garden.

"Didn't I tell you to stay away from me?" She tried to close the gate, and I hastily stuck my foot in the way. "What are you doing?"

"Come on, Blythe, you must have known I'd figure out you took the portal."

She didn't meet my eyes. "What are you talking about?"

"I know it was you," I went on. "The question is, why? I know you didn't realise the fairies had no need of the portal to get into this world, but you must have known the risk of bringing something you stole from a rival coven into Fairy Falls. Not just to yourself either."

Her hands fell to her sides. "That's your latest tactic? Did you run out of other people to accuse?"

"Look, I'm not going to report you to the police or anything." *Yet, anyway.* "I just want to know why you took it. You must have known Arabella would blame the fairies."

A long pause followed, in which her gaze remained averted from mine. "You know everyone had their eyes on that portal after word got out. If I hadn't taken it, someone else would have, and I knew how to keep it secure."

"What made you so sure none of the fairies on the other side would come out?" I asked. "Or did you not think of that part when you blew the cabinet up?"

She lifted her head, her cheeks pink. "I had to get the portal out of the cabinet to cast a spell stopping anyone from using it to get into the fairies' realm."

"You're lucky I didn't figure it out while the hunters were here," I remarked. "If they knew, they'd have blamed you for attacking Arabella too."

"No, they wouldn't have." Her flush deepened. "If the Inquisitor wants her dead, he's not going to let one failed attempt stop him from trying again."

She thinks the Inquisitor attacked Arabella. My lie-sensing power told me she believed every word she spoke, but that didn't change the fact that she'd kept me in the dark on purpose for her own convenience. Worse, she'd done the same to her sister too.

"Then the hunters will come back," I said. "They'll keep blaming the fairies for the theft as long as you refuse to confess. Did you know Steve wants to take away their citizenship because of this?"

She shook her head fiercely. "He won't. It's just bluster. Anyway, can you blame them for not wanting to come back?"

"No," I said. "I don't blame them for leaving, especially when you were happy to let them take the fall for your own crime."

"I didn't," she protested. "I tried to steer the blame towards those hunters instead. It's not my fault nobody sees them as a legitimate threat."

"Madame Grey does," I said. "You should have confided in her at the very least."

Another headshake. "She tries, but she won't be able to stop my mother from escaping. Not with the Inquisitor on her team."

I threw up my hands. "Can you try having a little faith in someone other than yourself? I'm going to take your word for it that you didn't mean any harm, but until that portal is back in Arabella's hands, the hunters aren't going to leave us be."

She backed into the garden. "Fine. I'll tell Madame Grey. It won't change a thing, though. The fairies want Arabella dead, and—"

A deafening screech, like that of an angry gargoyle, split the sky. I spun on my heel, alarmed, unable to see where the noise had come from. "What—?"

"I knew it." Blythe pulled the gate closed behind her. "I told you it wasn't over."

What's going on this time? I didn't stop to ask Blythe, and as I broke into a sprint towards the high street, several gargoyles rose in flight in a beat of their dark wings.

My path turned to the police station, from which Nathan and Erin had emerged along with some of the other security team members, and I skidded to a halt in front of them. "What happened?"

"There was an incident at the LPFP." Nathan's expression was even grimmer than it had been when the hunters had arrived, which was saying a lot. "According to Steve, there was a break-in."

"Or break*out*," Erin added. "The hunters called us for backup, so Steve sent some of his goons to help them. Whoever got into the jail had help from the inside."

My pulse surged. "You think the Inquisitor is behind this?"

"I'm almost certain of it," Nathan said. "Nobody can get into that place except people who already have security access. Steve also said the hunters were convinced it was fairy magic that bewitched the guards, though there's a lot of confusion over there."

The fairies. At least it all but proved that it wasn't *our* fairies who were involved, but the knowledge was bitter-sweet, given that Mrs Dailey would almost certainly be one of the escapees.

Steve shouldered his way out of the police station. "You lot—get back in here. Except you, Blair Wilkes. This isn't your fight."

"It's all of our fight," I told him. "I could have warned you this might happen if you'd been willing to listen."

"*You* need to shut your trap, Blair Wilkes," he said. "Where are those fairies of yours now?"

"They'd be here to help out if your hunter allies hadn't driven them away," I said heatedly. "I keep trying to tell you that the fairies aren't all in complete agreement. The ones who live in Fairy Falls hate the Inquisitor as much as the rest of us do."

At the word "Inquisitor," he bared his teeth, his skin greying as he began to shift into his gargoyle form. "We need to increase our security to make sure none of the runaway prisoners tries to get into Fairy Falls."

"That's the first good idea you've had all day." I knew that I was doing nobody any favours by needling him, but the thought of Mrs Dailey walking free—and what that would mean for her daughters—sent my thoughts into a spiral of dread and anger.

The grey spread further across his face. "That's enough cheek from you. Planning to chase after them, are you?"

"What would give you that idea?" The notion of staying put repelled me, but I knew I was no match for Mrs Dailey if she got her hands on a wand. Especially with the former Inquisitor on her team. I hadn't taken them as close friends, but he'd been running short on allies after his exile, and if he'd wanted to sow confusion among the hunters, what better way to do so than with a massive breakout from the most secure prison in the region? And what better way to gain the loyalty of the prisoners he set free?

"We're not going to chase after them," Nathan said. "We'll focus on keeping Fairy Falls safe."

"Yeah, I think the paperwork can wait until later," added Erin. "We'll tell Madame Grey."

"Good call." I took several steps away from the police station before I remembered. "Oh no. I left Rebecca there too."

"This is going to be rough for her, isn't it?" Erin said.

"Yeah… And Blythe, too, but I think she already knew something like this would happen. She knows how her mother's mind operates."

"Does she now?" Buck's tone was laced with suspicion. "Are you sure she isn't secretly planning to help her?"

"I'm sure, but she did have a secret inside her house." I might as well get it out in the open if Blythe herself had no intention of telling anyone. "Turns out *she* stole the portal, in order to put a spell on it so that nobody can get in or out of the fairies' realm."

"Blythe took the portal?" Nathan walked alongside me. "You know where it is?"

"It's at Blythe's house." I ignored Steve's blustering in the background and continued on my path away from the police station. "She didn't know the fairies don't need a man-made portal to get here, and neither does her mother."

"No kidding," Erin said. "You—don't want to go to the prison now, do you?"

"No, I don't know where Steve got that idea." My

hands curled into fists. "I want to keep them out of Fairy Falls, which means staying put."

We were too late to stop the breakout, after all, and I had no doubt Fairy Falls would be Mrs Dailey's first stop. As for the Inquisitor… I didn't know if he'd come, too, but revenge on me was bound to be at the forefront of his mind.

"What about the fairies?" asked Buck. "Can you send them a warning?"

"I wish I could." They were safer staying far away from the rest of us, but for all I knew, the Inquisitor would be able to find them regardless. Not that I knew what he was planning. The jailbreak had taken everyone completely by surprise—with the possible exception of Blythe.

Madame Grey was already waiting outside the witches' headquarters, her wand in her hand. "Blair—you heard the news?"

"About the jailbreak at the LPFP?"

"What jailbreak?" Her usual stoic manner gave way to unrestrained shock. "No—Arabella was attacked again. She's dead."

My heart jumped into my throat. "I'm guessing those two things are linked?"

"I imagine they are." Bleakness coloured her tone. "I warned Steve that something like this might happen."

My mind reeled. "It's got to be him. The Inquisitor."

"Yes, and I imagine Mrs Dailey was prepared for a while." She glanced behind her, where I glimpsed Rebecca cowering in the lobby through the open door. "I'll have to tell her children myself."

"Blythe should be on her way here too," I added. "She's coming to confess that she's the one who took the portal."

"Blythe?" She blinked, then the grimness returned.

"That would give another route for the enemy to get in. We have to remove it from her home at once."

"She put a spell on the portal so that nobody can use it," I told her. "Besides, the fairies don't need a man-made portal to travel from one realm to another."

"I see." Madame Grey's mouth thinned. "If that's the case, we need to secure the town in a way that we haven't needed to in a very long time. If you want to help, Blair, join Rita and follow her instructions."

She was prepared for this. Dazed, I found myself ushered into the lobby, where more witches gathered in groups of five or six. Rebecca was near the back, holding her sceptre in a death grip.

"What's going on?" she whispered to me. "Are Arabella's killers coming here next?"

"Possibly." She hadn't heard the rest, not yet, and we were running out of time. "Your sister's on her way here, so hang tight until then. We're going to secure the town's borders, right, Rita?"

"Yes," said Rita. "The boundaries are already warded against most outsiders, but there are certain spells that will prevent anyone from getting in at all until we're certain the danger has passed."

"Who's coming here?" Rebecca's wide eyes met mine. "Please… Tell me the truth."

I didn't want to underplay the issue, not when her life might depend on it. "She's coming, but we're going to keep her out."

"Then I want to help." She hefted the sceptre. "I know how to use protective spells. I've practised."

"It's too dangerous for you," Rita said to her. "I won't put your life at risk."

"But—it's faster and more effective to use a sceptre than a wand, isn't it?" she asked.

"Right you are." Aveline Hollyhock walked in, looking almost cheerful. "I told you you'd have to make the choice sooner or later, Rita. You, too, Madame Grey," she added to the witches' leader.

"Absolutely not." Madame Grey strode in front of the former Head Witch. "Rebecca, it's simply too dangerous for you to go outside."

Rebecca swallowed, gripping the sceptre. "Why did you make me keep this in the first place if not to use it?"

"Exactly," said Aveline. "Let her make use of her talents to defend her home."

"That's not for you to decide," I told her, though I had the sinking suspicion that she was right. A sceptre was so much stronger than a wand that if she helped set up defences around the town, it would both save time and spare us from having to coordinate every available witch or wizard to help… But what if Mrs Dailey showed up while Rebecca was exposed?

"It's up to me," she said. "I want to do it. Blair—you talked my sister out of taking me away from here, didn't you? Why is it any different if you're the one trying to tell me what to do?"

My mouth parted. "I'm not taking away your choice, but if you really want to do this, we need to be certain there isn't an ambush waiting for us on the other side of the town's border. Don't forget the escapees could easily have got here by now."

"Precisely," Madame Grey said. "There are too many unknowns. Arabella's attacker got away without even being seen, and given how fast the fairies can move…"

I racked my mind for a way forwards, and a light bulb flashed in my head. "I can watch from the sky and see if there's anyone trying to sneak up on the town. Glamoured or otherwise."

If the enemy was already here, it was too late, but if not, we had to act fast. I could only imagine the damage the former Inquisitor and Mrs Dailey could do to Fairy Falls, especially with an army of hostile fairies and escaped prisoners at their back.

I won't let that happen. No way.

Madame Grey gave me a long look. "All right, Blair. Go on."

"Right." I was nowhere near prepared to face either of our foes, but time was of the essence. I left the witches' headquarters and ran to catch up with Nathan.

"Nathan." I skidded to a halt at his side. "You haven't heard any more news?"

"No." He had his phone in his hand, but he and the others hadn't gone far from the police station. "Are the witches going to set up defensive spells around the town? Steve said they would."

"Yes—but Rebecca insists the sceptre is far more powerful than a wand," I said. "She's right, but she's facing pushback from pretty much everyone except for Aveline."

"I'm not surprised," said Erin. "Isn't she eleven?"

"Yeah, but she's adamant, and, well… We don't have a lot of time. Letting her set up the defences might be the difference between life and death."

"Yes, I can imagine." Nathan spoke in soft tones, his gaze searching. "You want to go with her?"

"No, I'm going to check nobody is sneaking up on us," I explained. "I can see through glamour, and it's easier to see threats from above than on the ground."

"True," said Nathan. "Don't put yourself at risk, though, okay?"

"I won't." I snapped my fingers and brought out my wings. While I could have used my Seven-Millimetre Boots, there were some things I could only see while in my fairy form. While I detected some sceptical looks amid the witches and the security team, I took no notice.

I was done being ashamed of who I was.

I took flight, soaring upwards until the cobbled streets and houses of Fairy Falls spread out beneath me. The glittering lake on the right, flanked by dark patches of forest, looked even more picturesque from the sky, yet there were too many routes from which enemies might enter our home. Gargoyles clustered on the western edge of the town while the security team covered the south. As I flew southeast, my gaze picked out a figure near the lake, outside the town's boundaries. Moving closer, I was completely unsurprised to see Thistle the elf tottering around, completely oblivious to the danger.

"Thistle, you have to move," I called to him as I descended. "The witches are coming here to set up defences around the town."

He lifted his head. "No, I have to meet my girlfriend here. I promised her."

"Seriously, Thistle, this is not a good time."

"It is," he insisted. "I found the ring. I can propose to Argyle after all."

"Oh, good," I said distractedly. "Go home and come back later when this is over. The hunters—"

"Yes, them!" he interjected. "The cabinet. I remember now."

"What?" My wings beat behind my back as I hovered on the spot. "If you remember who stole it, I already know."

"They tricked me, you know," he added, as if he hadn't heard a word I said. "They had their little friend put a spell on me, so I'd forget seeing them, but we elves are made of stronger stuff than humans are. I remember it all now."

"You… What?"

"That's right," he agreed. "We're consistently underestimated by humans, but that'll teach them, won't it?"

"What do you mean by 'little friend'?" *Someone put a spell on him? Not the hunters, surely.* Sleepy, Dopey, and Grumpy had even less magic than they had brain cells.

"That one, of course." He pointed upwards at a small glittering figure who hovered above the lake. *The pixie.*

"What?" The pixie had put a spell on him? As I straightened upright, the pixie vanished. "That… That wasn't the same pixie who helped me."

No. Other pixies had moved in, drawn by the fairies' return to town, and it had never occurred to me that there might be a spy among them.

Thistle shook his fist in the pixie's general direction. "You can't hide from me, my friend. I'll get you!"

"Not now, Thistle." I dragged my eyes away from the spot where the pixie had vanished. "You have to run. They're coming."

"Nonsense," he said. "Who's 'they'?"

A flash of light drew my gaze upwards, and my skin chilled. "The fairies."

15

T he brightness intensified into a purplish-white flare as I flew higher, leaving the elf behind at the lakeside. I *hoped* he'd have the sense to run for cover, because I couldn't do anything myself, not if the fairies were already here.

Not if *he* was here.

Several winged shapes rose into the sky, silhouetted against the fading light of the spell that had brought them here. My nerves buzzed as adrenaline flooded me. Here it was—proof that the fairies had never needed a portal to come in and out of this realm whenever they liked—and that they'd been watching us all along.

Whether Mrs Dailey was with them or not, I needed to stop Rebecca from leaving the witches' headquarters and exposing herself, but the fairies were already descending near the town's outskirts. One moved ahead of the rest, and a jolt of recognition hit me like a thunderbolt. While he and the other fairies shared the same pointed features, the same wings, and the same fine clothing that made him look almost unrecognisable as the man who'd worn sharp suits as the leader of the hunters—I'd always know his face.

Inquisitor Hare—or Rowe Clearwater—lifted his gaze to mine. "Blair Wilkes."

"Inquisitor." Fighting the instinct to flee as fast as my wings could carry me, I flew down to land in front of him. My gaze picked out five, ten, fifteen other fairies—some glamoured, some not. "I didn't know you were so short on allies that you decided to risk being caught in a jailbreak."

"You're as endearingly clueless as you ever were, I see," he said. "Allies are allies, no matter who they might be."

The blood surged in my veins. "You killed Arabella, didn't you? Why? Because she let the portal get stolen?"

"No," he replied. "Truth be told, I forgot she held it in her possession… one of the perils of living a long life. She was an inconvenience, however, and I suspected she would be a thorn in the heel of my plans."

His words held a surreal quality. I'd known intellectually that he wouldn't be idle while on the run, but I'd forgotten the raw terror of facing his calm calculation. This time I didn't hold a Seeing Stone to render him powerless, and I didn't recognise any of his allies either. They must have come from the fairies' own realm, and their abilities were unknown.

We'd only chased Clearwater off the last time because he'd been alone and cornered, but this time he was at the height of his power. My entire body trembled before him.

"What do you want with us, then?" I forced myself to meet his inhuman gaze. "Why are you at Fairy Falls?"

"I'm here to take back what you stole from me," he said. "And to ensure that your little town never stands in my way again."

The threat was clear. He'd take out anyone in his path —witch, shifter, elf, fairy, or otherwise. I scrambled for a way to stall him. "You want the portal? I can bring it to you myself."

I hadn't a hope of keeping him occupied long enough to let the witches set up their defences around the town, but Madame Grey had been prepared for the eventuality of his return. She must also have suspected he'd take us by surprise.

"You know perfectly well I care nothing for the portal, Blair." His gaze simmered with malice. "If you wish to turn your back on me, though, you do so at your own risk."

The other fairies fanned out behind him, some of them holding glittering wands, others raising swords. *Swords.* As if they'd walked out of a medieval novel. On top of the shimmering layer to my vision—glamour, on a level which I'd never faced before—I wasn't sure I could even trust my own senses.

"You're a fairy prince," I blurted. "Don't you have your own kingdom to rule over? What more could you possibly want?"

"I thought your father would have taught you about your kind," he said. "I suppose *he* hasn't dared go back to his own realm... too afraid of rejection from his fellow fairies, no doubt."

"Don't you talk about my dad." Anger writhed inside me, squashing my fear. "You rule over one corner of the fairy realm and you want to conquer the others, is that it? You want to be their supreme overlord?"

"Eventually," he said, without a hint of irony in his voice. "For now, I'll start by reclaiming the hunters—after I wipe your town off the map, of course."

Holy crap. He's serious. I reached for my wand as the

other fairies flew once again, too fast for me to track with my sight. A shimmering light flared up in the Inquisitor's hands, and an instant later, he held up a long, pointed staff. At its end, a purple stone glowed with luminescence.

"You took the sceptre." My throat went dry. "You— were you in Arabella's house at the last meeting?"

"No, but I had people watching. I always do."

The other fairies launched into flight as the Inquisitor lifted the sceptre. A bolt of purple lightning shot towards me, and I dodged, employing every ounce of fairy magical speed I possessed.

The spell hit the hillside, leaving a sizzling hole of burned grass in its wake. *Whoa.*

"You can't run forever, Blair." His voice pursued me, along with more flashes of purple light, as I flew left and right in a frantic effort to dodge his spells. I pulled out my wand with my left hand, and purple smoke billowed out of the end. I hadn't even had time to think about what spell I wanted to cast, but my instincts had taken over. More smoke poured out, clouding the air and masking me from sight.

I stopped to catch my breath and look for the others, but I'd obscured my own vision too. The lake caught my attention first, its surface reflecting winged shapes in the sky. Maybe it was the smoky haze, but it looked almost as if they were fighting… each other.

Squinting through the haze, I flew towards the water and recognised several of the fairies' faces. Those were *our* fairies—and they hadn't left the town at all. They'd come back to help fight off the Inquisitor's forces.

As more of the purple smoke cleared, the Inquisitor flew at me, lifting the sceptre—

"*MIAOW.*"

The booming voice shook the hill, and even the Inquisitor hesitated midspell. "What is that racket?"

"Sky?" I lifted my head. "Where—?"

A group of monstrous catlike shapes materialised on the lake's edge in a flash of glittering light. Sky, who was the biggest and fiercest of the lot, charged at the startled Inquisitor and forced him into flight.

Above, fairies' spells clashed like a fireworks display. When I recognised my dad among the new arrivals, my heart lifted. I launched upwards and caught up to him in the air, where he wrapped me in a hug.

"Blair," he said, his voice muffled. "Go somewhere safe —it's too dangerous out here."

"The Inquisitor has the sceptre," I gasped. "I don't know how he can use it, but—"

A bolt of purple lightning split the air, and Dad released me, his gaze dropping to the hovering figure wielding the sceptre. "It's me he wants. Blair, you have to leave."

"Both of us," I corrected. "He wants both of us dead, and I won't let you fight him alone either."

Even Sky wasn't invulnerable, despite his new allies— and Clearwater's threat had been clear. He wanted the whole town to suffer for what I'd done to him.

"I have experience fighting against my own kind," Dad said. "You don't, and it's too dangerous for you to be out in the open."

Around us, the other fairies flitted back and forth, firing off lightning bolt attacks. If I stayed out here, I was as likely to get hit by a stray spell as not—but the idea of leaving my dad in the middle of a battle was repellent.

On the other hand, I hadn't seen the witches yet, and if Rebecca had already left the safety of their headquarters when the enemy had arrived… I had to warn her. "Please be careful. I'm going to find Rebecca and make sure she's safe, but I'll come back."

"All right, but stay within the town's boundaries, okay?" He flew back, dodging another magical lightning bolt, while I glanced down to check on the lake. I hoped Thistle had taken my advice and hidden away, because half the bushes were burned to cinders.

Swooping leftwards, I kept the fairies in the corner of my vision as I followed the cobbled streets towards the witches' headquarters. Outside, I spied Madame Grey arguing with Rita.

"Blair!" Rita beckoned me down from the sky. "Have you seen Rebecca?"

I flew down to meet her. "No—isn't she here?"

"She and Aveline went off alone," Madame Grey told me, her gaze following the display of bright flashes of magic over the lake.

No. "The Inquisitor is here, and he said he's going to destroy the whole town. Did you manage to get any defences up?"

"No," said Rita. "That's what Aveline and Rebecca went to do."

"They what?" My heart jolted. *Rebecca.* "The Inquisitor has Meredith's sceptre. I don't know how he can possibly use it, but he wants total control over Fairy Falls, and he's fighting the fairies as we speak. Where are the other witches?"

"We have no intention of letting the fairies fight alone," said Madame Grey. "I sent reinforcements on their way to the lake and the other borders, but it was too late to stop Rebecca from leaving. I assume she and Aveline went north, avoiding the lake."

"I'll find them." I couldn't believe Aveline had dragged Rebecca out in the open in the middle of a magical battle, but Rebecca herself had wanted to use the sceptre to help, and Aveline had taken advantage of her frustration.

I won't forgive her if Rebecca gets hurt.

I flew north, wings beating as fast as I could move them. The streets below were strangely empty, and even the university campus was masked in an eerie silence. Nearby, however, I spotted two figures making their way to the northern border near the fence.

I zipped down and landed next to a startled Rebecca. "What are you doing, Aveline?"

"You know perfectly well what we're doing, Blair Wilkes," Aveline said. "Don't lure the fairies over here, fool."

"They can fly. It's not like they can't see you." Breathless fury choked me. "How long is this spell supposed to take? Where did you plan to hide if the fairies got here first?"

"One minute at most," Aveline told me. "As long as Rebecca follows my instructions and doesn't screw anything up."

"You're unbelievable. You're risking an eleven-year-old's life."

"For the sake of the rest of your petty little town, you foolish girl."

"She's right," Rebecca said. "Blair, this is going to be my last act as Head Witch before I give up the sceptre. Please let me do this."

"I…" I lifted my head and saw several winged figures flying over the forest. "I can't stop them all."

"You can at least stop distracting my sister." Blythe strode uphill, puffing from the exertion. "Let her cast the spell."

What? "You aren't going to smuggle your sister out of town?"

"No," she muttered. "No, I'm going to stop anyone getting in her way. Including you, if necessary."

I didn't even know what to think of her change of heart, but as the fairies' approach angled in our direction, all the arguments fled my mind. "You'd better hope the Inquisitor doesn't come back for that portal."

I launched upwards to meet the approaching fairies, who'd already seen Rebecca—but before they could descend on her, a tremendous roar arose from the trees, causing the fairies to stop midflight.

Werewolves.

They charged out of the forest, accompanied by an amalgam of other shifters—rats, wolves, foxes, badgers— and reared up on their hind legs to repel the encroaching fairies. Rebecca stared wide-eyed for an instant, but at a sharp command from Aveline, she bent over to listen to the elderly witch.

I have to trust her. I forced myself to turn my back on her and watch the werewolves drive the fairies away from the forest, but the battle above the lake appeared as chaotic as ever. I followed the fairies' retreat, eyes open for my dad, and my heart jolted when I saw the Inquisitor in the midst of the fray, sceptre in his hand.

He was fighting to kill, and the knowledge drove me into flight. *I have to keep him away from Rebecca.*

The closer I drew to the fight, the more the flashing lights blurred my vision. Blinking hard, I heard an unmistakeable roar from the lakeside. *"MIAOW."*

Sky. Heart in my throat, I flew towards the lakeshore, where my cat sat in his most monstrous incarnation. He and his huge shaggy beast companions bared sharp teeth and swiped at any fairy foolish enough to fly within reach, and when I neared, Sky's giant paw snagged my foot, yanking me out of the air.

He might be glamoured and not actually monster-sized, but it sure felt that way when he jumped on top of me. Winded, I lay flat on my back, pinned beneath his giant paws.

"Thanks for coming back for me," I breathed. "Please don't get yourself hurt."

"*Miaow*." I'd never heard Sky sound quite that murderous before, and I was immensely glad he was on my side as he reared up on his hind legs to swipe at the Inquisitor's allies. The fight had spread over the lake's edges, with the witches firing spells into the air while the elves ran around wielding pointed sticks. If not for the Inquisitor, we might have had a chance of winning, but with my cat sitting on my chest, it was a little difficult to move, let alone grab my wand.

"Sky," I said. "Can you please let me stand up? I'm no use to anyone while I'm lying down here."

Including Rebecca… and Dad.

"Miaow." Sky grumbled, but he lifted his paw off my body, enabling me to scramble to my feet. Not that I could see any clearer from an upright position. Fairies zipped around, while spells flew left and right in a sizzle of multi-coloured lights.

Then the Inquisitor appeared in the corner of my vision, his face screwed up in concentration as he took aim at my dad.

"No!" I screamed the word, snapped my fingers, and sent a glittering wind to strike down Clearwater from behind. It wasn't a powerful spell, but I'd thrown off his aim, enabling my dad to get out of the way.

The former Inquisitor turned towards me instead, raising the sceptre. A sudden glow ignited the air—not purple, but pure white—and pulsed above the lake. *That's not fairy magic.*

Without warning, Clearwater was flung upwards as if an invisible force had catapulted him into the air. His allies flew upwards, too, and my eyes picked out a rippling curtain of whiteness spreading rapidly over the lake and the forest. A barrier, encasing everything it touched, covering the town like a giant semitransparent dome.

Clearwater caught his balance above the dome, his face a mask of anger—and vanished in a flash of glittering purple.

"We can't let him get away." I flew upwards, only for Sky to grab my foot and pull me back to earth. "Sky—we have to catch him before he flees."

"Miaow," Sky said, meaning *he's already gone.* So were his allies, leaving a silence that was punctuated by angry roars from the werewolves and hisses from the fairy cats as they realised their quarry had gotten away.

The flashes of spells lighting the air petered out, while I saw several bodies lying on the ground below the newly conjured dome. We hadn't escaped the fight unscathed, and I went weak-kneed with relief when my dad flew from the other fairies to my side.

"Are you all right, Blair?" He pulled me close and then loosened his hold at once, surveying me as if assessing me for injuries. I didn't have any, and neither, to my relief, did he. "What spell was that?"

"I'm fine," I said shakily. "That… That was Rebecca, using her sceptre to put a protective spell over the town. It worked."

"I'm glad." He hugged me tighter. "I'm glad you're all right, Blair."

"He'll come back," I mumbled against his chest. "Please don't disappear again."

"I wish I could make that promise." He spoke quietly, but I caught every word. "If not for you, I might have stayed over there. Next time you should come with me. Clearwater won't be able to find us."

"I can't leave the others." Would I always be torn between two worlds? "Not even if he comes back."

We'd kept out Clearwater's forces this time, but the war was officially on.

16

It took several minutes for the news that the enemy had gone to spread through Fairy Falls. Amid the ensuing confusion, I went to find Nathan among the other security team members near the south border. When I landed at his side, he swept me into a hug. "Blair—I'm glad you're all right."

"Thanks to Rebecca." I indicated the shimmering dome covering the town. "Her sister decided to stay and help after all."

Rebecca had claimed that defending the town would be her last act as Head Witch, but there was still the question of what would be done *after* she gave up the sceptre. Especially if her mother came back. I hadn't seen Mrs Dailey amid the former Inquisitor's forces, but she was bound to be close by.

"She saved our necks," said Erin. She was wrapping a bandage around Buck's arm, which he held at an awkward angle. "Especially those of us who decided to fly without practising first."

"You didn't, did you?" I asked Buck, whose face

flushed. At least he looked uninjured aside from the broken arm.

"I wanted to help the fairies," he muttered. "They took a major risk by coming out of hiding."

"I know." I lifted my head to watch them flying over the lake, some carrying the injured, and my dad supervising.

When he saw me looking, he veered in my direction. "Blair, I'm going back into the forest to help the others," Dad said. "We won't be out of contact, not this time, so you don't have to worry."

"I understand." My chest tightened when I saw several bodies on the lakeshore. "Did anyone I know…?"

He shook his head. "No, they're the Inquisitor's people. I don't think he was worried he might hit his allies with that sceptre."

The sceptre. "I… yeah, we'll have to figure out a plan to deal with that. I'll send Sky to find you if I need you. Where is he?"

"There." Dad pointed across to a patch of bushes near the lake, where Sky had reverted to his ordinary cat form and appeared to be taking a nap. "Is Rebecca okay, do you know?"

"Go and check up on her," Nathan said. "Blair, I'll see you later, after we've cleared up some of this mess."

I wanted to help, but he was right. I wouldn't be surprised if Rebecca's sister had changed her mind and tried to smuggle her out of town, or else Aveline had tried to rope her into taking another risk. The security team had the cleanup in hand, though broken tree branches and debris littered the water and shores. The elves appeared to be collecting the former to use as weapons on their way back into the forest.

I took flight and headed north over the streets of Fairy

Falls, from which people had gradually begun to emerge from their houses. Witches filled the high street, but not Madame Grey. When I turned northwards, I saw her and Blythe in conversation near the fence to the university campus. She must have changed directions as soon as she'd realised who'd cast the boundary spell.

Rebecca herself stood rigidly, the sceptre clutched in both hands, and I landed beside her. "Rebecca—you did it."

She lifted her head. "Aveline ran off as soon as I cast the spell. She got past the border."

"She left town?" I echoed. "Is she mad? She'd have been safer in here."

"I imagine she knows the risks." Madame Grey approached us.

"Also, I won't shed a tear if she's the next one the Inquisitor murders," Blythe said in acidic tones. "She put my sister at risk."

"I told you, I made my own mind up," Rebecca said. "How long will the boundary spell last, Madame Grey?"

"I cannot give a definite answer," she said. "Ordinarily, the spell would only last a few hours, but with a sceptre… It might be weeks."

"Then we've won a fair bit of time," I concluded. "Who exactly does the barrier repel? I mean, can the rest of us leave?"

"It repels anyone who means us harm," said Blythe, without meeting my eyes. "That includes our mother and the hunters as well as those fairies."

"Excellent." I turned to Madame Grey. "And—the portal?"

"She knows I have it," Blythe said. "Don't get on your moral high horse again."

"That's not what I was trying to do," I protested. "That

portal leads into the Inquisitor's own part of the fairy realm. It's also a potential bargaining chip."

"Hardly," she scoffed. "The fairies don't need portals to get in and out of their realm, but humans do, so I'm not going to hand it over to someone who might give it straight to my mother."

"The local fairies will be happy to take care of it," Madame Grey said. "They'll also no doubt be interested to know how you rendered the portal inoperative."

Blythe flushed. "I doubt they would. It's a witch spell."

"You'd be surprised." I turned back to Madame Grey. "We have to do something about that sceptre. The Inquisitor—how is it possible for him to use something designed for humans?"

"He likely tampered with it," said Madame Grey. "But fairies' magic is not greatly different from our own, especially for those who've lived in both worlds."

I swallowed, feeling a mixture of shame and vindication. If our types of magic were incompatible, I wouldn't be able to use both witch and fairy magic myself—but that fact had enabled the Inquisitor to access unimaginable power. "I bet he's going after the hunters next. His allies already broke into the prison, so he's probably killed anyone who opposes him."

"Not necessarily," she said. "A mass slaughter would have drawn too much attention. He has powerful glamour at his disposal, and a number of other fairies willing to do his bidding. I can imagine an enchantment would have been more efficient than simply murdering his adversaries."

"But... Does that mean he can make the hunters forget he ever deceived them?" She didn't need to answer that question, and the notion was somehow worse than him simply murdering his adversaries outright.

How could we hope to go up against the entirety of the hunters' forces *and* the Inquisitor?

"They should have been prepared," Blythe said. "He's been on the run for ages, and they ought to have known he'd come back."

"Maybe some of them were prepared." It would be nice to imagine that some of the hunters were ready to oppose their former Inquisitor, but that didn't mean they were on *our* side. "Oh no. I forgot to ask Nathan. Most of his family works for the hunters."

Blythe made a disparaging noise, while Madame Grey inclined her head. "Yes, I imagine he's preparing to contact them. Most of us are going to have to make difficult choices."

No kidding. Rebecca knew that better than most, and from the tense way she gripped the sceptre, she didn't seem to have resigned herself to giving it up just yet. Maybe because Aveline had fled town. *I bet she ran off to avoid facing the consequences of what she did.*

"Not yet," Blythe said. "Rebecca, do you want to go home?"

"No," she said. "I want to talk to the other witches. I bet they have questions."

"They do," said Madame Grey, "but I can answer them. You deserve to take some time to yourself. You don't owe everyone an explanation."

"Exactly."

I heard rustling in the nearby trees and spied several shifters returning to the forest. The werewolves' Chief would have questions, too, and so would the elves, but Rebecca had already done her part. I'd gladly talk to them myself if it meant sparing Rebecca any further strife.

"I could say the same to you, Blair," said Madame Grey, as if she'd sensed the direction of my thoughts. "My granddaughter is helping the injured. She'll be relieved to know you're alive."

"Oh yeah." Alissa would also be relieved to know that Aveline had finally vacated our flat, despite the former Head Witch's sneaky disappearance. "I'll find her. See you later?"

"I'll call for you when I need you," said Madame Grey.

"Sure." I reached out and put an arm around Rebecca, careful to avoid knocking the sceptre out of her trembling hands. She accepted the hug with a faint whimper, which told me how much she needed the comfort.

"Don't listen to your sister," I murmured to her. "You don't have to be strong all the time."

"I know," she whispered. "Thanks, Blair."

Blythe scowled and didn't say goodbye, but I ignored her. I hoped she'd get over herself and share everything with Madame Grey that she'd been hiding, but that was her own decision to make.

In the meantime, I flew southwards and to the hospital. Alissa stood in the entryway, and when I landed in front of her, she gasped. "Blair. You're not hurt, are you?"

"No, and I have more good news," I said. "Our unwanted guest is gone. She sneaked out of town after Rebecca put up the boundary spell."

"Seriously?" Her brows shot up. "Rebecca did that all by herself?"

"With instruction from Aveline," I said. "Who ran off to avoid the consequences of making an eleven-year-old responsible for protecting the entire town."

"Typical."

"We have our flat back, though," I added. "Sky will be pleased too."

"He's back?"

"Yeah, he spent half the battle sitting on me," I said. "He was napping by the lake the last I saw him."

"I saw the fairies too," she said. "They're back?"

"For now," I said. "Even Madame Grey doesn't know how long the defensive spell will last, and the Inquisitor—Clearwater—is still out there."

She sucked in a breath. "You must have been terrified."

"Honestly, I'm not sure I've even processed it yet," I admitted. "He has the sceptre, he helped Mrs Dailey break out of jail, and he's probably going to take the hunters back under his control. How can anyone figure out how to handle all that?"

"My grandmother will think of something. She always does."

"I hope so." There would be no going back to normal from this, not for a while. The outcome could have been much worse, but it was horribly jarring to see the streets of Fairy Falls filled with shocked civilians—witches, shifters, fairies, and countless others.

Alissa stepped back as someone carried an elf with a broken leg into the hospital. Thistle. At least he'd escaped the lake, though he didn't look too happy.

"I should go and help out in there," Alissa said. "See you later?"

"Of course." I needed to tell Nathan about the Inquisitor's intention to take over the hunters, if he hadn't already guessed. Aside from Erin, none of his family members had ever liked me, but they were still his relatives, and he'd hate to see them put under a fairy's spell.

I left the hospital and flew south then changed directions when I saw Nathan and the rest of the security team walking towards the police station.

"Blair." Nathan halted to wait for me to fly over. "The

witches cleaned up the mess at the border in a few seconds. Everything okay?"

"Are you going to check in with Steve?" I asked. "Wait—what happened to those gargoyles who went to help the hunters at the LPFP?"

"That's what we'd like to know," he said. "Steve hasn't been able to get hold of them. And—and Erin is worried about the rest of our family."

"I wondered if you'd guessed." I lowered my voice. "I know you aren't close to them, but Madame Grey thinks he's more likely to use glamour to bewitch people into helping him out than anything... worse."

"Exactly," he said. "I'll have to find out who was present at the LPFP at the time, but the former Inquisitor might go after the branch near the Knotgrass Coven's house before he targets the branch where my family works."

"Yeah... I hope you're right." We'd lost too many people already. "She's dead. Arabella is. He murdered her... And I never managed to stop him."

"There's nothing you could have done to prevent that, Blair," he said softly. "We can't keep everyone safe."

"I know, but the Inquisitor... He'll be furious we drove him out of Fairy Falls." Grim certainty lay beneath my exhaustion. He'd want to get back in, or lure me out of town, and Nathan's family were still on the outside.

"Exactly," he said. "Erin is calling our dad, but it's anyone's guess as to whether he and our brothers will listen or if they'll just assume we're exaggerating."

"I hope they do listen." That might be too much to hope for, but the seriousness of the situation might win out.

After all, we'd only forestalled the inevitable. Eventually, we'd have to meet the other fairies in battle again.

While Nathan returned to the police station, I was too

restless to go home like Madame Grey had told me to. Instead, I returned to the lakeside to pick up my cat and found he'd already gone. The other fairies had too. Assuming I'd find Sky back at home, I flew around the forest and saw an incredibly odd-looking pair approaching one of the paths. Blythe walked in the lead, awkwardly carrying one end of a giant mirror. Holding the other end was the second of the strange pairing—Vincent the vampire.

I swooped over to them, too curious to leave them be. "Hey, Vincent. Erm… What are you doing?"

"Giving this back to its owners," Vincent supplied, jerking his chin at the mirror.

"The fairies." I swivelled towards the forest. "Do you know where to get into their realm? You can't see through glamour."

"No, but you can," said the vampire.

Had he been hoping I'd show up? Blythe couldn't see through glamour either, though she remained reluctant to meet my eyes.

All right, then. I flew ahead of them and into the woods. Relief washed over me when the transparent path into the fairies' part of the forest became visible.

"Remarkable," said Vincent, looking over the top of the mirror at the flickering path. "How intriguing."

I couldn't tell if the vampire was being sarcastic or genuine, but the path looked exactly the same as usual, as if it had never been gone. I walked ahead, my heart lifting.

Sky met me near my dad's cottage, greeting me with a miaow, and I crouched down to stroke him. "Is Dad in there?"

"Yes," Dad answered from behind him. "What—is that the portal?"

"It is." Conor stepped in front of me. "You again? I hope you've come to apologise."

"Don't be ridiculous," Dad said. "It's not Blair's fault. I'm the one Clearwater wanted to get to. Besides, it looks as if she's brought our property back."

"It's not our property." Conor's glare landed on Blythe and Vincent, though the vampire's bared teeth made him tone it down. "It's Clearwater's."

"The portal is sealed so it can't be used, right, Blythe?" I raised my voice, seeing that the other fairies had come out of their houses to watch. Rosalind and Ani were among them.

"Right," Blythe muttered, not making eye contact. She looked as if she wouldn't mind vanishing into the portal herself, though I was surprised she'd volunteered to carry it back.

"Good," Dad said. "I think your house is the safest place to keep it, Conor. Don't you agree?"

Conor paused for a heartbeat before relenting. "Yes, I suppose. Bring it this way."

He beckoned, and Blythe and Vincent followed. For some bizarre reason, the vampire shot me a wink over his shoulder before they walked out of sight.

"Vampires." I shook my head. "I don't know why he volunteered to help Blythe."

"Maybe he wanted to see our home," said Dad.

"He can read my cat's mind whenever he likes, though." I scratched Sky behind the ear. "Sky, I have good news. We have our flat back."

"Miaow." He padded after Dad into the cottage, and I walked behind him, happy to get away from the attention.

"Wait, you do?" Dad asked as I closed the door. "That Head Witch—she's not staying?"

"Aveline ran out of town earlier," I explained. "To

avoid the consequences of pressuring Rebecca to save everyone, I think."

"Ah." He sat down in an armchair. "Wise of her, I think. Rebecca took on a huge burden, though she's the reason we're still alive."

"Yeah." I sat down, too, and Sky curled up in my lap. "This isn't over, though. The Inquisitor is going after the hunters, and Madame Grey thinks he'll use glamour to bewitch them into forgetting what he is."

"I thought so." He appeared unsurprised, but he'd seen Rowe Clearwater's capabilities for himself. My dad knew more about our foe than the rest of us did. Maybe even Madame Grey.

"What are we going to do, then?" I shifted in my seat, and Sky grumbled at being disturbed. "There's so many more of them than there are of us, and he has the sceptre too."

"He does," he agreed, "but it's not infallible, and neither is he. Don't forget we can get into the fairies' realm too. My own home isn't off-limits."

"You—you can?"

Sky lifted his head and miaowed an affirmative.

"Yes, of course," he said. "Whether my former home is safe or not is another matter. It's been so long that my old allies might send me packing immediately."

"Might," I echoed. "You're saying there's a chance they'll help us?"

He nodded. "Yes, I think it's time. Blair, would you like to meet your other fairy relatives?"

ABOUT THE AUTHOR

Elle Adams lives in the middle of England, where she spends most of her time reading an ever-growing mountain of books, planning her next adventure, or writing. Elle's books are humorous mysteries with a paranormal twist, packed with magical mayhem.

She also writes urban and contemporary fantasy novels as Emma L. Adams.

Visit http://www.elleadamsauthor.com/ to find out more about Elle's books.